PRISON Fans

A Book Of Short Memoirs, Including An Exclusive Interview With An Incarcerated Online Adult Entertainer From Inside His Prison Cell, And Conversations With Convicts About The Different Types Of Lust and Romance Experienced Behind Prison Walls.

PRISON Fans

A Book Of Short Memoirs, Including An Exclusive Interview With An Incarcerated Online Adult Entertainer From Inside His Prison Cell, And Conversations With Convicts About The Different Types Of Lust and Romance Experienced Behind Prison Walls.

MALIK IBN LEROW

Contents

This book is dedicated to the women who love a man regardless of his circumstances and to the stand up guys who had to sit down before they became even better men.

LOADING

LOGGING IN

Have you ever wondered what goes on behind the walls of a prison? Have you ever wondered what goes on inside those steel and concrete cells? Or how the men keep their sanity after being sentenced to 10 years, 20 years, 30 years or even for life? What's their motivation to live in these circumstances? Are the prison rape stories true? Do they feel love? Is there any romance? Can a woman fall in love with a man in that place? Is a man even human after being confined over a long period of time? The interviewer in this book attests to a lot of things after serving over a decade in various prisons, but at the same time, he only speaks for himself because every situation is different. The disposition of each individual determines how the prison environment affects him or how he affects others within this setting.

The interviewer presents to us stories of inmates with varied dispositions behind prison walls. These stories are told by the seducers and predators imprisoned after they were found guilty of committing heinous crimes. Each story is unadulterated. And even though the answers to the questions asked above may surprise you, the fact remains that the human race is affected by incarceration just as much as it is affected by crime. In a world full of insatiable lustful curiosities evidenced by the overhaul of subscriptions to Only Fans, it would only be right to give you a means to feed your curiosity regarding prison life through the pages of *Prison Fans*. Brace yourself- You are now subscribed.

AN INTERVIEW WITH MR. ROCKHARD

On a return visit to the prison, the interviewer ran into some familiar faces, one of them being Mr. Rockhard. They served time together over a decade ago in a different prison. Since the last time they met each other, the interviewer has enjoyed the benefits of being free, but Mr. Rockhard has not. He is now on his 28th year of incarceration and will be maxing out his 30-year sentence soon. It was imperative for the interviewer to document this legendary story of how Mr. Rockhard brought adult entertainment to the cellblock and made a living as an adult entertainer on the internet while serving a 30-year sentence in the Georgia penal system.

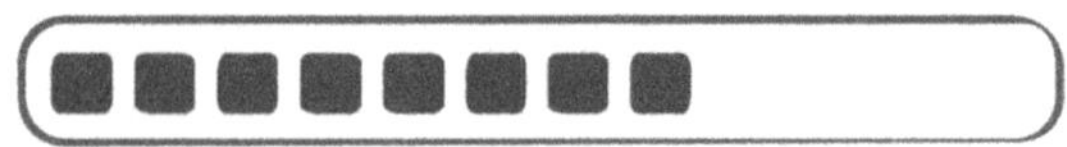

MR. ROCKHARD: This my brother I was telling you about *(showing Instagram profile)*, so he make 1000s and 1000s of dollars doing this right here; look, look at him!

INTERVIEWER: Is this big bro or lil bro?

MR. ROCKHARD: We are a year apart, but I'm the oldest. I'm a year older than him.

INTERVIEWER: Ok, you're a year older than him — cowboy da real body rocka.

MR. ROCKHARD: Yeah, everybody. Everybody know him, you know…any woman that like this type of thing knows about him. You say the name Cowboy. They gone be like yeah! That's the man.

INTERVIEWER: *(laughs)*

MR. ROCKHARD: We started doing this thing together, man! We started a long time ago, a long time ago.

INTERVIEWER: Are you talking about 90's, like early 90's?

MR. ROCKHARD: We were young. We were so young that we couldn't tell the promoters how old we were because they wouldn't let us work. We wouldn't get the job. So we had to say okay man! I'm 21 now man, but we were only 15-16.

INTERVIEWER: Wow, so how did you start in prison?

MR. ROCKHARD: How I started out in prison? I was looking at people like them females, like Melissa Ford, Buffy The Body 1. I would look at girls like Esther Baxter, girls that do the videos. You know the video girls who were making all this money but they weren't really doing nothing and didn't really look like nothing, and just wasn't really nothing too much. So I learned the game from them. So I've seen how everything went from actually being in the show to being on the internet. So I say oh, okay, I can get on the site and do a virtual show for the women. On the site that you can get paid right then and there leading up. So you got sites like Peek, Tagged, Bigo, sites likes Mico. You got all these sites, man, that you can really do whatever on the screen and people pay you through gifts or they pay through Cash App. You can put your Cash App on the screen and they can pay me like that so I got an idea. I said okay, let me start going in and start banging a little bit harder, working out a little harder, and getting the outfits together and promoting a little bit. So I started working out real hard you know, doing reps in place. What I did was I went on these sites and I just went live first without even saying it out loud. So I asked, "if I started doing you know, giving y'all a little strip tease show because you can't get all the way naked, would y'all like it?" And they were like, "yeah yeah". So I looked around to see what the other dudes was doing. So I went shopping around and seeing what other dudes that's you know, trying this on the internet was doing and I seen that nobody was doing, you know, saying 30 minutes show 20 minutes shows for the women on these sites. All men would do is just sit there talking or they might be in a gym working but I saw that nobody was actually doing dance shows for the women. So since I come from a dancing background, it was perfect.

INTERVIEWER: And the rest was history.

MR. ROCKHARD: That's how I got my start from my dancing background. I've did a show for Mary J Blige, I'm on some videos on YouTube when I was young dancing in Luke videos. I come from a dance background but that's why I know a backup dancer don't make no money. You see Chris Brown on stage, you see Usher on stage, you see these folks on stage, Cierra on stage, them folks dancing in the back don't make no money. They might work in a grocery store, fast food restaurant, or some like that. The sort of dancers that made the most money out of the male dancers are the strippers. They make the most money hands down out of any kind of dancer you can think of. I don't care who you see him on stage with. You can see him on stage with Michael Jackson. They don't make no money but the strippers are making the money, a lot of money!

INTERVIEWER: Are you referring to live or online strippers?

MR. ROCKHARD: Whether it's live or digital. The Internet making more money, than anything right now because of the pandemic and people don't want to catch anything so people trying to distance themselves. Another thing is people might want to look at you in the privacy of their own home, instead of being put out there. A woman thinking like I'm a doctor. I'm a lawyer. I'm a public figure. I can't be seen at a male review. She'd rather just sit behind the computer in the home and just pay you like this. Throw their dollars by punching the keyboard or touching the screen. Do what you do but whatever you do, you got to make sure you do it good. You gotta make sure you practice; you got to make sure you know how to spread the moves out, and don't do the same dance moves over and over- you gotta learn how to spread it. I had to learn how to do that because a lot of strip shows that you go to on the street, male reviews dancers don't be up there but for about 15 minutes. I started doing shows for one hour. So I had to have seven eight different songs and I danced to the whole song. But I had to do something different. I had my outfits where I know that with this song I actually take & rip the shirt a little bit then take it off but this song I do this and that song I do that. I had to map it out. I had to map that thing out.

INTERVIEWER: Wow! Man, that's amazing. You did all of this live from the chain gang?

MR.ROCKHARD: I used to sit my phone right here, *(indicating area on prison cell sink)* and I can call somebody right now. I'ma call a female that was at every single show I ever did and she will explain how it used to go. You want me to call her?

INTERVIEWER: Yeah!

MR. ROCKHARD: *(He calls his biggest supporter and places the call on speaker)* Hey are you busy, you busy? I'm doing an interview on how I got started with the shows so we want you to give like an overview of how it used to start and what used to happen in the middle or end your like your favorite part or whatever.

FEMALE: You want me to say something?

MR. ROCKHARD: Yeah go ahead.

FEMALE: It was like a striptease. He would be like excitement for the women and they will like throw gifts everywhere and they loved the excitement of him doing his little striptease show.

MR. ROCKHARD: Tell him about how it was in prison and it was just one area.

FEMALE: Yeah, it was like basically one area of the room and he would get all on the floor and everything and it was really amazing. He was like secured in that one little area that nobody didn't know that he couldn't do too much of everything.

MR. ROCKHARD: Okay, okay, now what was your favorite part of the show? Was it like the part where I will lick my tongue in the screen or how I did the chair?

FEMALE: Unh unh! When you rolled your um body.

MR. ROCKHARD: Was this the chair or did you just like when I rolled my body really close to the screen?

FEMALE: I liked the chair too.

MR. ROCKHARD: Okay, so tell him about the chair.

FEMALE: You would stand in the chair and you would roll your body in the chair, acting like you'rehaving sex with the women and everything.

MR. ROCKHARD: Hey I appreciate that. I'ma hit you.

FEMALE: Yeah *(call ended)*.

MR. ROCKHARD: *(continues)* What I used to do. I'll sit my cell phone just like this *(indicating toward the prison cell sink)*. First I'd go live and ask, "Y'all ready, Y'all ready?" I'll have music playing on the phone. All the music was straight off my phone. I didn't have to have no other phone. I did everything from one phone. So I'd ask, "Are y'all ready? I'ma give y'all five minutes to get ready, to go get your money. I'ma give y'all 5 minutes to do all of that." So the music would be playing and I'd really be getting dressed and getting rigged up. We're talking about stripping so I gotta say this, no homo stuff, but in the club or male reviews, the male strippers have to rig up so what we do is take our wood get it right and take like elastic and tie the back of it, tie the middle, and then tie the top real tight then take a sleeve and put it on top of your wood, then you put you clothes on top of that So it's sticking out and don't never go down and never go down until you take that off. It goes the whole time until you take the rig off but you got to catch it right you got to get it in there at the right moment or it won't look like nothing. This how dudes stay up the whole time. But you gotta tie the base and you gotta tie the top. You gotta do both of them. So I do that. I do my lil thing. I might have a tank top that a cut a whole lotta holes in or something like that and I set it up like this here (indicates to phone propped up on prison cell sink) and I get out the screen so they don't see me nobody sees anything but this same plain white wall. Then once my intro comes in, I have an intro made and everything, then I come on the screen and do the whole show from right here (indicating small area in front of prison cell sink). If I have a chair. So I put the chair in the room right here (indicating area in front of prison cell sink). I have a part where I get on the floor. I take the phone and prop it against the wall on the floor. And I get on the floor right here. And I have parts where I roll, roll roll on the floor and stuff like that. And the women used to be going really craaazy!

INTERVIEWER: Dope, how many used to view you.

MR. ROCKHARD: I used to get like, sometimes I used to get like 5,000 views. These be 5,000 women in there at that one time well at least I think they was all women. I don't know.

INTERVIEWER: *(Burst into laughter)*. Yeah yeah yeah viewers!

MR.ROCKHARD: 5000 viewers, and they all throwing money.

INTERVIEWER: That's dope, that's dope. Yeah man that's dope!

MR. ROCKHARD: You got to look at what you do good man! Just because you in prison don't mean that you can't keep going, you know, improvise and make it your own. So the woman respect,like she said, the women respected the fact that I was locked up and I was still was doing this for them, doing something different for them. They respect the fact that you know he locked up and he still being entertaining for us you know, and they liked it. They supported it and they'd be supporting me to this day if I was to start the shows back now. I'd get the same support.

INTERVIEWER: So you're retired right now?

MR. ROCKHARD: Not really. Not really. I'm just on something else.

INTERVIEWER: Ok yeah yeah yeah.

MR. ROCKHARD: Because if the opportunity present it-self, I was actually thinking about starting back doing it with the Mico App. I was thinking about doing it. Because the Bigo App was a little strict. I can't really take my shirt off or they'll ban me. I've seen that with the Mico, you can get away with anything. So I was thinking I might or can do a little 15-20 minute. I don't have to do the hour I can do like 15-20 minutes. And the women gone come in they gone do what they do because still ain't nobody really doing it yet. You know, not on these apps they still not up on it yet. It's an untapped market right now for dancers. Since this pandemic thing, they're not seeing everything on the internet. And they keep trying to do it on IG and stuff but they really not getting paid. They need to go to these other smaller apps and bring their crowds to the smaller apps and get paid. So it's still an untapped market their not even looking at.

INTERVIEWER: Mmmmmm!

MR. ROCKHARD: They can make 1,000s and 1,000s of dollars in 15-20 minutes.

INTERVIEWER: So basically we have more time and bet-ter ideas come to us sitting right here?

MR. ROCKHARD: Right. I would have never man. I got my brother's one of the major strippers out there right now. He never did prison time. He was like this, was mind blowing to him. When I told him how I was making virtual shows in prison, and he said man are you saying what how you come up with that? What made you think about it? I said man, you in prison man, you sit down you either gone do one thing you gone be better or you gone be worse. It's your choice. If you choose to be better. You gone sit down you know, and think of some type of way, some type of way to be better. You tired of being broke. You're tired of selling drugs. You're tired of doing all this stuff, man that keep bringing you back to prison, you get tired of it. So then you gone think uh, what can I do? What can I do to still generate money man, because you know, I like nice things. I don't want to be struggling. So what can I do? You gonna come up with some idea. So that's how we always come up with being in here.

INTERVIEWER: So how often did you do the shows?

MR. ROCKHARD: So yeah, I used to live for this show. I did it three times a week. I did it Wednesday, Friday and Saturday. I did it back to back on Friday and Saturday because that's the best time we have that's good, but at a camp like this! See that's what really made me want to start back because I'm looking at how this, man, I can do a late night show man, at like three o'clock in the morning man. My roommate don't care about nothing. He'll stay in another room for two or three days man, he don't even care. He don't complain. I can actually have the same area. See, I was just at Leesburg in a six man cell. You never got no time. I'm back at a camp like this, 15-20 minutes boom, boom, boom, boom, boom. But I really my mind ain't really into it right now.

INTERVIEWER: So you say the ladies used to get mad and send hate mail because you had to cancel due to emergency count or the prison was on lockdown for a stabbing and stuff like that?

MR. ROCKHARD: They'd get mad, they'll be angry. I used to get hate messages.

INTERVIEWER: So the ladies will be like, No! We want our show, we want our show, you're gonna lose me as a *fan (laughing)*.

MR. ROCKHARD: I'ma tell you the craziest thing I got a hate mail for, one time I was doing the show. It was so many women in there throwing gifts. My phone froze up then it went out.

INTERVIEWER: Noooo!

MR. ROCKHARD: When it went out then when I got back on, I got a lot of inboxes from women telling me, "you ain't shit"," You did that on purpose," "You ain't a good entertainer." I'm talking about bashing me! But I had a lot of women tell me the opposite. One of the best thing I heard was a female telling me she was feeling down. She was thinking about committing suicide all this crazy stuff about herself and that once she started seeing my shows, it started to give her something to look forward to. And she came up out of all that depression. She say it motivated her- this man in prison, he is really good!

INTERVIEWER: Mmm!

MR. ROCKHARD: See, the thing about it is this. I'm in prison and I put my heart into what I did. I was really entertaining wasn't like no, because a lot of people see I actually go to other people live and stuff. I'd say y'all come check out my own striptease, and they just think it was like a comedy thing. They think it's like a joke. Like somebody gonna come in and be able to laugh and say hahaha, that type of thing. But when they came in and seen it was a real show, and women would see that I was doing real dance moves. It was really like it was really organized when they seen that. When they seen that bro man, they become a fan, they get real serious, and it became like a real show like no joke. At first, people say oh, you stripping man, you ain't stripping, Ima come through, but they be like like chomping it off, and they mess around and come and get locked. Now they like, "When is your next show? How can I get you to do more? Can I pay you for a private one? Can I do this? Can I do that?".

INTERVIEWER: So it opens other doors as well?

MR. ROCKHARD: I'll say it open all type of avenues and people saying, one person for example said I'm a scout for the "love after lockup show." They wanted to put me in that but I had too much time left. I could call the girl who was going to play my girlfriend because a lot of them, people don't really be together for real. I can call a girl right now that was gonna play my girlfriend on love after lockup. But when they found out I had too much time left and I couldn't do it because you got to have a little bit of time so they can film it up to when you're getting out but I had too much time left. All that came from doing the shows. All of that came from that, a lot of opportunitie., I met a lot of people. Got a lot of supporters. A lot of people want me to start it right now. They want me to start it right back up.

INTERVIEWER: You think you can perform like you did before or you might be a little rusty?

MR. ROCKHARD: I'm in the same shape. I dance exactly the same. I could do it. I look exactly the same. I might actually got more followers.

INTERVIEWER: I know it's some hate that comes with this. Who were your biggest haters?

MR.ROCKHARD: I got a lot of hatred from the men. The men was my biggest haters.

INTERVIEWER: Oh that's gone be with anything that happens anyway.

MR. ROCKHARD: Sometimes women will see you so much that they'll paint a fantasy in their head. Like, they're in love. They will actually fall in love from seeing you like this and they don't even know you. So a lot of the hatred that came from the women. Is that they will fall in love from what they see but when they try to get to know me, they see that I'm not really looking for a relationship. It's just a show then they'll get mad. But they made themselves mad.

INTERVIEWER: Yeah, exactly.

MR. ROCKHARD: You know, I'm an entertainer, just like if you go the movies to watch Denzel Washington and during the movie you fall in love with him. You can't get mad because he married, you can't get mad because he don't want to go out with you. You fell in love with the image of him on this movie and so they fell in love with the image of an exotic dancer on the screen during a live show done virtually on the internet. So when you get in my inbox and I don't respond, like you think I should respond and you say can I get your number? And I said no, or something like that. You can't get mad at that.

INTERVIEWER: Other than being disinterested, is there another reason you don't like to give out your number?

MR. ROCKHARD: Because I've been burned before. I done gave girls my number from doing the shows. Man, they find out my name, where I'm at, call the folks. I done been through all that type of stuff.

INTERVIEWER: Wow!

MR. ROCKHARD: Them girls will call the prison. I done had a officer come to me saying, look somebody done called and said you a stripper on the internet. I'm just letting you know man, we ain't gonna come shake you down, but I'm just letting you know someone just called down here and said that.

INTERVIEWER: Wow!

MR. ROCKHARD: A lot of the male's be haters. A lot of male's was the majority of my haters because they'll hear their girls talking about it or whatever, so what they'll do, and I know it because you can tell a fake page when you see one. The men will come in with a fake page and leave a lot of negative comments. But see you as an entertainer, you have to block a lot of stuff out. I can't be bothered by stuff like this during the show. Because sometimes in the middle of my show, I might stop and read the comments and ask questions like, "did y'all like that or do y'all want me to do more of that? Alright I'ma do it again." And I'll step back and do some more of what they like. I can't be or it'll be unprofessional of me to see that I see the negative comments and be like oh, "Man, fuck you Janice89 you ain't nothing but a bitch anyway!" That's just gonna take away.

INTERVIEWER: RIGHT.

MR. ROCKHARD: So I had to block all the negative stuff out. I done had fake comments coming in saying, "Oh y'all get this prison nigga outta here stupid ass ho's!" Shit like that or, "You can't dance,"stuff like that, you know, a lot of negative stuff. I had to over look all of that. You gotta block it out. You gotta take the good with the bad. I take the good comments. Love em, I take the bad comments too. But normally, you know a lot of time boy them girls throw so many gifts and comment, so much that you might see a negative comment come in on the screen and it don't stay on there a half a second before it's gone.

INTERVIEWER: *(Laughing)*

MR. ROCKHARD: "Bitch ass nigga" it's gone. Because the girls. I'd say I got majority. I say I got 90% love and 10% hate. 90% of it was love. I'd be sitting up here faking if I just say I had a whole bunch of haters and just a lot of hate. You see, when I called ole girl she ain't said nothing about the negative. She said the women loved it. And this and that this and that. It's a sexual thing for the women. You know what I'm saying.

INTERVIEWER: Right.

MR. ROCKHARD: A lot of women can be comfortable in their home and don't have to worry about who watching them and get that same satisfaction. However, they do. If they masturbating pleasing they self or they just like watching. Or they get together with a group of their friends and they like watching it together. However they used to do it. Man them girls used to be on point as soon as I started announcing them shows. They used to flood in there in a matter of seconds. 200, 300, 400, or 500 in seconds. It'll go up, go, go ,go. Then it'll go down a little bit. Then it'll go back up. That's how I used to do it.

INTERVIEWER: So you're saying the ladies might have Mr. Rockhard on a 72 inch screen TV on the street having a girl's night party.

MR. ROCKHARD: And I did all that in prison and it changed my life.

INTERVIEWER: *(Laughing)*.

MR. ROCKHARD: I didn't have no help, matter of fact, I got a partner man. He's at a halfway house right now who was with me along the whole way. Matter of fact, I can call him and ask we can get his view of everything. Watch this. Let me text him real quick. He probably, he might be at work and he might not.

(Mr. Rockhard makes call on speaker phone and guy answers)

GUY ON PHONE: What's up bro?

MR. ROCKHARD: Are you busy?

GUY ON PHONE: What you got for me?

MR. ROCKHARD: I need you to do something for me right quick.

GUY ON PHONE: What's up?

MR. ROCKHARD: You're on speaker. We're doing this interview right about the tagged thing I used to do. I want you to just give a little overview of what you know about how I used to do the live shows and the reaction I used to get from the women on the show.

GUY ON PHONE: You say what? Now I can't really hear you.

MR. ROCKHARD: I say I want you to give, we doing an interview, and I want you to give a little insight of what you know or what you remember from the reaction I used to get from the women from the shows I used to do on tagged.

GUY ON PHONE: All right.

MR. ROCKHARD: Go ahead, go ahead right now.

GUY ON PHONE: Used to get like 90% of good reactions and 10% bad. You know you gone always have some haters. It was 90% good reactions. Umm just umm, very umm, what you call it what's the word I'm looking for, entertaining you know. It was good, so much goes on, he need to go back to it.

MR. ROCKHARD: (*Laughs*) I might try it, I might try it on the Mico man! I might try but I used to get pretty good reviews from the ladies right here from in prison right? That's the main thing in prison you know! what I'm saying doing these things from in prison.

GUY ON PHONE: That's the best thing though. That's what they like. You feel me! They motivated for the show to keep going you know.

MR. ROCKHARD: Right right right!

GUY ON PHONE: It was up to them for it to keep going.

MR. ROCKHARD: Right, exactly. Alright, preciate bro. I'ma hit you back.

GUY ON PHONE: Alright, love.

MR. ROCKHARD: That was just off the top. I ain't have to coach him on what to say so like the majority of everybody loved it. It was a big thing. It wasn't no small time thing. I can call numerous people man and they'll say the same thing. They gone say, "Oh yeah, man. He was doing he was actually doing real shows. It was a real thing it wasn't like he was just messing around playing. No, it was serious. It was professional. It was- I was getting paid. I was cashing out.

Interviewer: *(Laughing)* You was cashing. Ok yeah man.

MR. ROCKHARD: But it was a lot of hard time and determination I had to put into this. I had to put all shyness to the side. You in prison and you know, you got a lot of people that was in prison on Tagg too. So a lot of dudes was seeing me, you know… a lot of dudes was telling me man! I came to holler at you on your live and boy you was in there dancing.

INTERVIEWER: *(bursts out laughing)*

MR. ROCKHARD: I'd say oh yeah. Yeah yeah yeah. But a lot dudes inside the prison, besides the Muslims it's a different thing with them, but a lot of the regular dudes they respected the hustle. They looked at it like man bro hustling a whole nother way man hustling a whole other way. That's how it went.

INTERVIEWER: Wow man! Yes, that's definitely definitely dope news.

MR. ROCKHARD: I think I got a picture from it bro. You'll laugh. I know I got one somewhere. I think I got a screenshot from the actual show that one of the girls took and sent to me. I know I got one somewhere.

INTERVIEWER: I know it's something you left out what else you ain't tell us?

MR. ROCKHARD: I used to do the show sometimes from the shower. Prison shower. I used to take my pants and my belt and I used have my pants like this and I used to loop my belt around the bar. I used to stick my phone in my back pocket where the camera will be hanging out and I'd do the whole show from the shower. Just like that.

INTERVIEWER: *(laughs)*.

MR. ROCKHARD: The whole show from the shower.

INTERVIEWER: Very creative. Improvising at its finest.

MR. ROCKHARD: You gotta make it man, gotta run that sack up.

INTERVIEWER: Gauge it. You know what I'm saying? Pre-record ,gauge it ,see where the camera showing, make sure it's lined up right and go live.

(MR. ROCKHARD FINDS A PHOTO)

MR: ROCKHARD: This this at the beginning when it was at 72 views this one of the pictures right here look at the comments,"Yas", "Rock","Ooh", "sexy","Take it off baby"

INTERVIEWER: (bursts out laughing)

MR. ROCKHARD: That's at the beginning, you see, I still got my clothes on, I just started it. I had just clicked it on. You see how many diamonds I had that's like 1 million right there, it's a lot you know, saying? That's how I cash out. And this was the beginning of one of the pages, this was one of the new pages I made

INTERVIEWER: Okay okay.

MR. ROCKHARD: I have to look deeper for some other screen shots from the girls who screenshot and screen record to show me their favorite parts. I see it and let them know I appreciate it.

INTERVIEWER: Yeah for sure.

MR. ROCKHARD: I have to say a lot about appreciating it, thank you, because I'm real humble man. They didn't have to support me. They didn't have to do that. They could have said aww! He in prison man whatever. But you can't have those type of thoughts. You can't entertain the thought that I'm in prison man ain't nobody gonna feel me. If I would've had them type of thoughts, I would have never been successful in it. Never! I said okay man, if I put my heart and my time, and my effort into it man, it's going to turn out right. And that's what it did.

INTERVIEWER: If the ladies want to follow you and get a peek at your content where can they find you?

MR. ROCKHARD: They can follow me on Instagram- *mr_ rockhard850*

AN INTERVIEW WITH JACK GAME

This ain't New Jack City and it's not a robbery. At least not a carjacking or anything a normal civilian would think when it comes to the Jack Game. Becoming a product of your confinement is similar to becoming a product of your environment, and you'll see exactly what I mean after this interview.

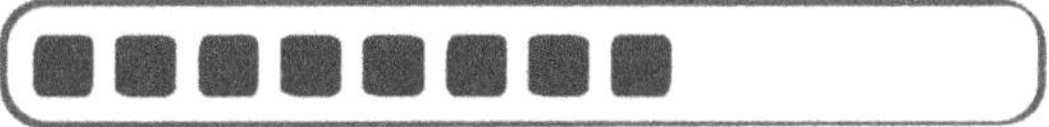

INTERVIEWER: My man, so tell me, how did you get the name Jack Game?

JACK GAME: The jack game, well you see, I got the name Jack Game because I'm the honorary ambassador of the jack game. See in prison it's a game that you'll have to be here to understand it.

INTERVIEWER: Okay, well, see. We trying to give the people a better understanding of you know prison, so I mean tell me, let me know what it's like, what is the jack game?

JACK GAME: Well, first of all you got to know the lingo so jacking is jacking of or masturbating you know, so in prison we have to do what we have to do to satisfy our sexual urges the best way we can. So some people do homosexual activity and some jack. I chose to jack and I represent for the jack game, it's a community of jackers we're a community and I'm the honorary ambassador.

INTERVIEWER: *(chuckles)* Honorary ambassador of the jack game?

JACK GAME: Yeah, yes I am. I'm the honorary ambassador.

INTERVIEWER: So tell me, how did you get that status as the honorary ambassador? Jack Game: Well, you know, it's etiquettes and rules to the game. You can't just be claiming the jack game if you ain't going by the rules.

INTERVIEWER: Break that down for me.

JACK GAME: See, you got different type of jackers, some that follow the rules and some that don't follow the rules. The ones that don't follow the rules they ain't real jackers. You know, they might jack but they ain't in the jack game. See, you can't be squirreling and be talking about you in the jack game. Nall ain't no squirreling going on man, if you in the jack game. You got to be out there and let them folks see it they got to see you. If you really in the jack game, she need to see you.

INTERVIEWER: Wait a minute. What you mean? What's squirreling?

JACK GAME: Oh, you see squirreling. You know how a squirrel moves when he's after a nut or gets a nut. He's moving cautious and scared like always prepared to run away or jump back in the tree. So when you squirreling – you sneaking and jacking your dick. See you sneaking and peeking, you know, when the officer or the lady or whoever you're seeing to jack on. You peeking you know what I'm saying you ain't letting her see that you're jacking but you getting off on her. For example, you in the shower and the lady come in to count or she come in to pass out mail or you in the hole and the nurse coming around for pill call or whatever the case may be. You looking out the door and when she turn her head, you jacking your dick off the back of her head or the back of her or she get somewhere where she can't see what you doing but you looking at her jacking your dick. Nall man that's squirreling, you gotta let her see that thang she gotta know that you jacking because you really want her to eat it up and that's the chance you gotta take in the jack game where either she gone scream on you or eat it up. Because hey, it's a lot of women that eat and they not gone just come to you and say that you gotta try it and see.

INTERVIEWER: Wow!

JACK GAME: This is what we do in the jack game you know, not only are we jackers, we're also feeders because we feed the ones that's hungry. The women who got a job at the prison because they like to eat. They come to work hungry and the jack game serves them well because we gone give them plenty meat to eat.

INTERVIEWER: Hold on man. You said a lot right there okay, eating? What the hell is eating?? What do you mean she like to eat???

JACK GAME: Listen man, listen, you act like you ain't never been to prison before. Listen, when she eating, that means she likes the fact that you jacking on her, she likes seeing you jack, she likes to see you jack your dick. That's what you call eating. A lot of these women officers they be monsters. They get these jobs and that's the highlight of their day, to come to work and see some dick, and what I do is I make sure they see it. And anyone else in the jack game gone make sure she see it too.

INTERVIEWER: Okay and what happens if she screams on you?

JACK GAME: When she screams on you that means she calls you out or writes you up for jacking. Usually they'll try to embarrass you or have you put in the hole, sometimes you just get written up, and sometimes she just tells you not to do it.

INTERVIEWER: So basically if she screams, that means she doesn't like to eat?

JACK GAME: Most of the time but not always, a lot of them are sneaky and have their picks. Just because she let me get off don't mean she'll let you. And sometimes depending on whose around her when you're jacking will make her scream because she don't want another officer, staff, or inmate to know she allow it. It don't be the fact you pulled your dick out on her. It be how you went about doing it mostly.

INTERVIEWER: Damn so it's an art to it?

JACK GAME: Yeah, man. You can't just pull your dick out. I mean you can, but things can turn out bad for you when it's disrespectful to others in the environment. The more reckless you are, the more you'll go to the hole, get in fights, or even get a free world charge. It's a lot of experiences and adventures in the jack game.

INTERVIEWER: Oh yeah, tell me about the experiences and adventures of the jack game.

JACK GAME: Sometimes you have to test the waters so when you come out, you might see it's a new officer, some young fine officer and you don't know if she eat hell. She don't even know because sometimes you have to turn a female out to the jack game. They don't even know they like it until you turn them out to the jack game. So sometimes you taking a chance on going to the hole for pulling your dick out on this lady. At times its some really bold moves made in the jack game. For example, if I'm able to catch that young officer in the booth alone and I want to turn her out, I might get butt naked on the big floor and give it to her with the grease while she ain't never seen or expected such a display. And if she scream or call them people ain't no sense in stopping. I may as well keep going until I bust my nut and go on to the hole. Ain't no sense in stopping. I'm gone get mine off whether I go to the hole or she eat.

INTERVIEWER: What about the other inmates? Do you just get naked in front of men and all??

JACK GAME: No, it's not like that. You see, when I do something like this, I usually have on a robe with nothing on under it in the very early morning or late night when nobody is really up and outside their cells. And the few that are up, I'll tell them what I'm about to do so they don't be looking.

INTERVIEWER: Damnnn man that's some crazy shit. Ain't that like a pedophile or a sex crime or something? So they just send y'all to the hole for that?

JACK GAME: Yeah, they write you up and give you what they call a B-11 and you go sit over in the hole or whatever, man. It is what it is when you're doing time that's how I do my time- I jack.

INTERVIEWER: I'm assuming B-11 is like a prison code or something right?

JACK GAME: Yeah, the department of corrections have like their own laws or rules where you get a citation for breaking them. They charge you $4 for each write up you're found guilty of and you get put on like store, phone, or visitation re-striction as like a form of punishment for violating the rules. You can plea out or go to Disciplinary Report Court and try to beat the charge but it's unlikely that you will.

INTERVIEWER: And you don't care nothing about none of that?

JACK GAME: Nall man, I make my commissary off the land shining boots and writing for the jailhouse lawyers. I don't get visits and I don't have money on the phone so I don't care if I get wrote up.

INTERVIEWER: What you be charging for your services, how does that go?

JACK GAME: So I shine boots for two or more soups depending on how much of the boot a person wants shined. If they just want the tip of the toe shined ,that's two soups or an equivalent store item. If they want more of the boot shined, I charge more. Now as for the law work, I charge a soup per page. I have good hand writing so dudes that be fighting their case or working on other people's cases pay me to write the briefs and motions for them or what not.

INTERVIEWER: So what's some other wild experiences that come with the jack game?

JACK GAME: Man, I'm all on the walk with this man. I got masks for me to get away with it. I'll be on the walk with my sock and be ready to take somebody down I'll have my mask on and go hit the store lady.

INTERVIEWER: What!

JACK GAME: Yeah, I'll go get in the store line while they running store and I'll get to the back of the line and just kinda watch the store lady. I'll see the store lady right there and I'll see it. I see it in her eyes that she want something that she wanna get something. And just in case so I can get away. I keep a lil mask that I can put on in my pocket. I'll wait til the time presents itself, then once it present itself, I'll put the mask on, turn the corner, then boom! give it to her right then and there just whip out and start jacking.

INTERVIEWER: This is wild bro.

JACK GAME: It's like a rush. It's like a thrill that I get when I do this. You know what I mean? It's exciting.

INTERVIEWER: Well, I don't know what you mean but I hear you.

JACK GAME: And sometimes the rewards come too. I had an officer that was so hooked on me that whenever she was in the booth by herself, we had us a session. I'm talking about we had a thing we did every day. Every day at a certain time when she come to work man.

INTERVIEWER: Unbelievable!

JACK GAME: Believe it. My cell was directly across from the control booth at the time. So what I'd do is when she come to work, she'll sit at the desk and I'll be in my room and when the officer that's working with her leaves her by herself. She'll start looking straight across in my room. And I would get butt naked and put on a show for her while she play with herself and put on a show for me too.

INTERVIEWER: How did she put on a show for you?

JACK GAME: Eating food like bananas, yogurt, and sucking on blow pops. Stuff like that.

INTERVIEWER: I'm just not getting how y'all do this in front of everybody?

JACK GAME: In prison there are unwritten rules like mind your own business and respect the gun line you know.

INTERVIEWER: The gun line? You mean like from the movie Life?

JACK GAME: *(chuckles)* Yeah, something like that but if you cross the gun line or the jack line, you will get shot down by some dick.

INTERVIEWER: Oh hell! nawl *(Laughing)*.

JACK GAME: Yeah man, so if you see a door cracked open or angled towards the booth or in the direction of some female- that's the gun line. And at times you'll be warned if you happen to cross into the gun line if it isn't too late. A lot of times people get shot down unintentionally and don't even know it.

INTERVIEWER: Damn! *(laughs)*

JACK GAME: Shit happens!

INTERVIEWER: Okay, so when you'd did your thing with the officer chick you had a gun line?

JACK GAME: Exactly. So since I had the very first cell on the end, I could open my door as like a block to 95% of the dorm. And everyone knew not to walk that way when my door was opened. The other 5% of the dorm was secured by the officer because she had to open the dorms main door from inside the booth in order for someone to cross the gun line from the left side.

INTERVIEWER: Oh ok, so ya'll had a professional operation going on, I see.

JACK GAME: I told you, I'm the ambassador of this shit.

INTERVIEWER: Yeah, that is right *(laughing)*.

JACK GAME: Man I've built relationships with females like that where they'll bring me food and boxers with their fluids in it , the whole nine yards straight off the jack game.

INTERVIEWER: Straight off the jack game hunh! Jack Game: Yeah, man a lot of these women be freaks. They be wanting to see me, they be wanting to see dick. Just like men wanna see pussy, they wanna see dick. Some females embrace it and some don't but I can honestly say I done had my fun. I keep some grease.

INTERVIEWER: What you say man, you keep some grease?

JACK GAME: Yeah, I gotta keep some grease that's mandatory in this game. I even have special attire for certain occasions.

INTERVIEWER: Jacker outfits?

JACK GAME: If that's what you want to call it but I already told you about the robe. I also have pants with no crotch or big rips or holes in them for quick and easy access.

INTERVIEWER: On site?

JACK GAME: That's right I stay prepared to get down on site. Could be in medical with the nurses or in the classroom so it has to be easy access in those settings and some of the women let you do your thang. Majority of them will let you do your thang and don't be trying to scream on you or nothing like that. A lot of them respect it because you're not engaging in no homosexual activity and you're getting off the best way you can. So I do what I do.

INTERVIEWER: What's some other tips and tricks of the trade?

JACK GAME: So if I really want to be sneaky and get off on someone I know gone scream on me. What I'll do is, I'll tie a string on my dick on one end and tie the other end of the string to my toe. That way, when I tap my foot on the ground the string will jack me off. No hands.

INTERVIEWER: You kidding me?

JACK GAME: Nall.

INTERVIEWER: I thought squirreling was against the rules??

JACK GAME: This is an exception to the rule. I'ma tell you what else I do. I keep me some type of candy, some type of coffee and stuff like that man. You know that way, I get my most. I feel it more. I get more erect so in the process, I might have some honey or jelly on my skin somewhere that I can lick it. So I'll lick the honey while I'm doing my thang and looking at my target.

INTERVIEWER: So you put honey on….. you know what never mind.

JACK GAME: Yeah, it's a jack thing you probably wouldn't understand but I like to engage all of my pleasure senses to increase my arousal while I jack.

INTERVIEWER: Damnnn bro! So if them folks let you out right now. You know that shit a crime on the street, you can't be jumping out pulling your dick on people. You know that don't you?

JACK GAME: Oh yeah man, I don't think I'll have that problem since I'll be back and have access to women to satisfy my desires. So it'll be different from being locked up but at the same time just to add a little novelty with somebody that wants it, ain't nothing wrong with watching each other masturbate. Sometimes that can be like a fetish or something different to add into your repertoire. So yeah, I wouldn't risk getting in trouble or coming back for that. This is just a prison thing for me.

INTERVIEWER: Yeah man, because somebody will kill you about their wife if you get out and pull your dick out on a man wife or daughter. Somebody gonna kill you.

JACK GAME: Yeah man, I know. But hey man, it is what it is. People do things that can get them killed all the time. It's a lot of things that people will kill you for out there so you just gotta stay safe man. And do you- be you.

INTERVIEWER: So I see you being you with this hair. How you get it to slick back and wave up like that? Almost thought you was pimpin with a perm a first.

JACK GAME: I come from a long line of game members but it's a little secret. I use to keep them for bothering me in here. You know they only want your hair 2 inches or less in here. I use shampoo and a lot of grease when I get in the shower and just comb it in to the roots, let it stay in and when I get out the shower, I comb it back and brush it down then I tie it down so once it drys, it locks.

INTERVIEWER: Well, there you have it, how to give yourself a perm in prison.

JACK GAME: That's right.

INTERVIEWER: Alright Jack Game man, keep your head up and we'll see you on the other side.

JACK GAME: No doubt.

LOADING

AN INTERVIEW WITH FIGHT OR FUCK

*I*n this interview, you will get into the mind of a man that confirms and expounds on the saying, "Don't drop the soap." Fleece Johnson is a household name representing the aggressive type of homosexual. That is, a predator inside of prisons as he's always lurking and looking for fresh meat. Booty meat. But this guy, he goes by the name of Fight or Fuck, and even if you fight, sometimes you still get fucked.

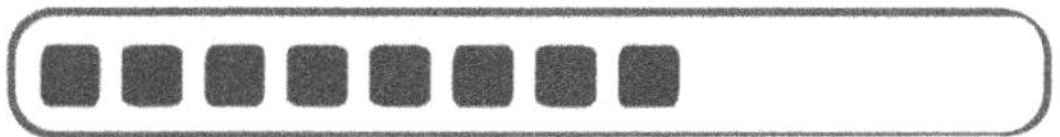

INTERVIEWER: Fight or Fuck. That's a helluva name. How'd you get that name?

FIGHT OR FUCK: Well, it was a something that an officer said to me when I first came into the prison. He said, "You gone fight or you gone fuck." So once I got in and found my true self, I become the embodiment of the saying, "Fight or Fuck".

INTERVIEWER: And how did you do that? How did you become the embodiment?

FIGHT OR FUCK: First, I want to say when a man comes to prison, his sexual desires come with him. So when you got a bunch of men in one place and they all horny, they getting hard, and majority aren't going home, no time soon if they go home at all. And there aren't no type of conjugal visits allowed with a woman, all they have access to is each other. "What you think gonna happen?"

INTERVIEWER: The first thing that comes to mind for me is a lot of masturbating.

FIGHT OR FUCK: That can be true for some but for me that's not enough. I'm gone get me some ass.

INTERVIEWER: How do you go about getting some because I'd assume that guys aren't just giving their ass away?

FIGHT OR FUCK: Believe it or not, nowadays guys are giving their ass away more than ever but when I started my bid back in the 80's, it was more of a predator/prey sort of thing. For the most part if I liked someone, it was because they reminded me of a female in how that looked, moved, or talked. And when I like someone, I'm gone get in their butt whether they want me to or not.

INTERVIEWER: Damn you tuff!

FIGHT OR FUCK: Yeah, I let them know that I want them and they can go about giving me what I want the easy or the hard way. They can fight or fuck but most fighters make for a better fuck. I'm undefeated.

INTERVIEWER: Never lost a fight?

FIGHT OR FUCK: I've lost some fights but I never lost a fight for some booty. You see a fight for some booty is like a fight for survival. It's like food and water, I gotta have it. I love getting in a man's butt so it's very important to me.

INTERVIEWER: I know that back in the seventies and eighties, homosexuality wasn't accepted like it is now. You didn't feel any shame having sex with a man?

FIGHT OR FUCK: Ain't no shame in my game. I'm not ashamed to admit what I do. Some people committed suicide but I adapted and lived to tell the story so I'm not ashamed of it. A lot of people won't admit what they did inside of prison but back then taking booty was a trend that a lot of the toughest guys were a part of.

INTERVIEWER: Where are the officers at when all this is taking place?

FIGHT OR FUCK: Officer's? Man you're on your own in here, especially back in the eighties in Alto. Practically nobody was safe, even the officers. Hell, I done slapped a few of them on the ass.

INTERVIEWER: Wow! Tell me about Alto.

FIGHT OR FUCK: Awww man! I got a lot of stories from Alto. Alto is where I got my stripes and learned the ins and outs of being a booty bandit.

INTERVIEWER: Is that what they call it?

FIGHT OR FUCK: Yeah, back then that's what it was either you were a booty bandit or your booty was up for grabs. Booty bandits were like a crew of ass takers, so if we caught you slipping, we'd throw a sheet over your head, choke you out, and when you woke up you'd have someone up in you.

INTERVIEWER: That's Vicious.

FIGHT OR FUCK: And we'd run a train on you.

INTERVIEWER: Sheesh.

FIGHT OR FUCK: While I'm getting my turn, the other guys will pin the victim down and we'd rotate until we get tired.

INTERVIEWER: No mercy?

FIGHT OR FUCK: None. Once we gotcha and believe it or not a lot of the victims become willing fuck boys after. It's like they lose their mind and start tossing ass to everybody. It's like they grow to enjoy it or something. Like how a female get turned out and be buck wild, you know.

INTERVIEWER: I find it hard to believe that y'all can't get in trouble for this. C'mon, now keep it real.

FIGHT OR FUCK: I never said you can't get in trouble. You can get in a lot of trouble and potentially get a lot of extra years on your sentence but what's more than a life sentence when you already got one?

INTERVIEWER: You might have point there.

FIGHT OR FUCK: And most times, the dudes gone be too embarrassed to tell and if he tell, now he a snitch. So it's just doesn't end well either way.

INTERVIEWER: I heard snitches get stitches.

FIGHT OR FUCK: For sure and then I was laced by old convicts on how to get away with it even if they do tell. Anytime I hunt a man myself on a solo mission, I also make him put the grease in his ass himself. That way, he will have grease under his finger nails just in case he decides to run and tell afterwards.

INTERVIEWER: What does that do?

FIGHT OR FUCK: That's like evidence that he consented because it'll be my word against his. So I'm gone tell the people he been my boy because I take care of him, I been fucking him, and he wanted me to fuck him because he greases his ass up for me every time.

INTERVIEWER: So you make the man put grease on his own booty hole?

FIGHT OR FUCK: Not just on his booty hole, I make him finger his own ass and like loosen it up too.

INTERVIEWER: Damn it man! So when you go on a solo mission, how do you get them to comply?

FIGHT OR FUCK: Well, it's a few different ways I can tell you about, but I'll start with fear. You ever had somebody surprise you in your sleep with a homemade shank or sharp metal rod in your ear?

INTERVIEWER: Never.

FIGHT OR FUCK: Well, that's what I do. I'll give him an option to have me shove the metal rod through his ear hole into his brain or take my dick up his ass. I let him feel the point of the rod sticking inside his ear and make him decide right then which one he wants. They always pick pleasure over pain.

INTERVIEWER: I think you would've had to kill me.

FIGHT OR FUCK: You don't have time to think. You only have time to react to the unexpected situation and nobody wants to die for real. I also knock guys out, pull them in the room, and take the booty.

INTERVIEWER: Sneak attack!

FIGHT OR FUCK: Ain't no fair one in hunting. You ever see a lion tell a gazelle he about to eat him?

INTERVIEWER: Nall.

FIGHT OR FUCK: Alright then. So I'll catch a white boy walking down the range or near my cell door and knock him clean out. When he wake up, I might have him in the buck with my tongue in his ass.

INTERVIEWER: Ain't no way.

FIGHT OR FUCK: I turn them white boys out especially the blondes.

Interviewer: So wait a minute, you discriminate by race?

FIGHT OR FUCK: Majority of the time I go after white boys. I've had some black booty but it wasn't forced.

INTERVIEWER: Why do you mostly target white boys?

FIGHT OR FUCK: Well, a few reasons but it's the power. I like how it makes me feel to break a white man down and make him submit to me like a woman. Its like a role reversal from how they take advantage of us in the free world and target us unjustified, you know.

INTERVIEWER: That's some cold blooded activism right there.

FIGHT OR FUCK: And on top of that they have a more feminine look with the hair and colorful eyes. They rarely fight back and are easy to scare like a woman. Man, I'll never forget this white boy came in the system trying to act black, sagging his pants, and all. It was crazy because everything about him made him sexy to a booty bandit like myself, but he thought it would keep us away. My partner and I really enjoyed him.

INTERVIEWER: What did he do to make his self sexy?

FIGHT OR FUCK: For one sagging your pants under your butt is like flirting or inviting someone to your booty just like passing gas around a man.

INTERVIEWER: Passing gas like farting?

FIGHT OR FUCK: Yeah, if you farting around a man letting him smell your ass that's like flirting with him or letting him know he can get some of your ass.

INTERVIEWER: Damn!

FIGHT OR FUCK: Yeah, so this young white boy had like longer than normal blonde hair, blue eyes, pale white skin, with no beard. Sagging his pants. I had to have him and within 72hrs, I had him. My partner and I caught him by the TV- sagging. I come from behind, grab him and put the knife to his neck. I'm close up on him so I can feel his ass on my dick, I tell him, "I'll put this knife in your neck crack, don't ever be out here advertising my ass like that." My partner come from the front and put the knife to his face and we take him to a cell. We get in the cell and the white boy is so scared. You can see him shaking. He begging, "Please don't kill me, please don't kill me." I tell him, "Shut the fuck up and take them pants off." He pull everything down, pants and boxers. My partner leave out to watch the door. I give the white boy some Vaseline and baby oil I got mixed together in a jar and tell him to grease his self. Like I said before, I always make them grease their own ass before I penetrate them just in case they scream rape. So after he grease up I go in him slow. This virgin ass so it's tight- real tight. The white boy moaning like a bitch saying how it hurts so bad right. So I pull out, put some more grease on and start fucking him. My partner hit the door, saying he trying to get right too. So I get off the boy and stand outside the door. My partner go in and slay him- the white boy hollering. We took about 2-3 turns a piece on the white boy before we finished so the boy ass bleeding, he crying and shit. Long story short, the white boy had to go to the hospital and had my partner and I caught up in a rape investigation.

INTERVIEWER: Damn! How did that go?

FIGHT OR FUCK: So the next day they had came and locked the building down. Put crime scene yellow tape around the cell we fucked him in and took my partner and I to the hole. They put us back there pending investigation. Of course, we denied the accusation and they was unable to corroborate his story because he took a shower a few times before he went to medical and he still had grease under his fingernail. We stayed in the hole about 60 days until they shipped us to separate prisons.

INTERVIEWER: That was a close call. Did you have any other situations like that?

FIGHT OR FUCK: I've had different situations but not quite like that one. I kind of calmed down on the aggressive type rapes after that and started to finesse booty. They made it more easy for you to catch a charge or get put on high max with that PREA stuff.

INTERVIEWER: I know high max is like permanent lockdown in a room by yourself for 23hrs with 1 hour recreation. What is PREA?

FIGHT OR FUCK: Yeah, so that's the Prison Rape Elimination Act which basically has the prisons set up now where you can call a hotline from the wall phone and report harassment or rape without having to tell an officer or leave the dorm and they respond immediately. It's kind of like crime stoppers for booty bandits.

INTERVIEWER: Oh! They got some for your bad ass now *(laughing).*

FIGHT OR FUCK: Not really. If I really want to, I can still take some ass but it's just too easy to have to go through drama behind that when I can just finesse. Nowadays a lot of these dudes come in the system gay and bisexual anyway, so it's easier to just finesse. I'm more of a booty finesser these days.

INTERVIEWER: And how is this finesse executed?

FIGHT OR FUCK: Well, it's different ways but I'll start with the guys who come in the system and they don't have nothing. They don't go to store, they don't got no family support, no food, no cosmetics, no hustle or nothing. He just sitting in here with nothing so what I'll do is, I'll take care of him. I'll feed him, make sure he got some soap and stuff but in return, he gotta be my girl and give me some ass.

INTERVIEWER: Damn! So dudes let you hit for commissary?

FIGHT OR FUCK: Unwittingly yes. You'd be surprised man at how many guys eat the honey bun that I put on their bed to have to turn around and let me spread their buns.

INTERVIEWER: Trick em and trap em

FIGHT OR FUCK: Yessir it's all in the game. Once their in debt they owe you whatever you say they owe you and if they owe me I want to be paid in booty.

INTERVIEWER: Gots to be more careful.

FIGHT OR FUCK: And other times they don't necessarily be broke or in debt. They may have a lot of money and family support but they are weak and afraid. These types are like the bottom of the food chain and can easily be gang raped so with me having a name and respect in the system I let these guys know that as long as they belong to me nobody will mess with them. This will limit their vulnerability to being robbed or gang raped by submitting to me and only me as what we call a War Daddy.

INTERVIEWER: War daddy….. wow!

FIGHT OR FUCK: Yeah, see, I'm the aggressor, I'm the one who's going to stand up so you get the picture. The name is self-explanatory.

INTERVIEWER: So you'll go to war over some booty?

FIGHT OR FUCK: Hell yeah! When I got a boy, he is like my girl. People die every day about booty on the street so it's no different in here. Many people have been stabbed and killed about messing around with the wrong boy. If someone tampers with my product, it's going to be a problem.

INTERVIEWER: Product? Is your boy for sale?

FIGHT OR FUCK: I wasn't saying it like that but at the same time, I have pimped a few boys out before.

INTERVIEWER: So you're like a wayward pimp?

FIGHT OR FUCK: Yeah man, so you know one of the convicts might ask me about the boy and I'll let them know. If they make an offer I can't refuse, which they always did, I'll let them rent some time in the boy.

INTERVIEWER: How did you get paid?

FIGHT OR FUCK: Well, before I tell the boy, he has a date and send him out to handle the business. I always received advanced payment via Western Union, commissary items, or both.

INTERVIEWER: Purse first, Ass last! *(laughing)*

FIGHT OR FUCK: You know the game and that ain't all. We used to have real sissy boy entertainment and what I mean by that is we'd get the boys dolled up and let them prance around the dorm, dance on table's for store items, and if you wasn't with it, you'd just go in your room.

INTERVIEWER: This is hilarious. How you doll up a man in prison?

FIGHT OR FUCK: It's really simple, especially when the female guards are cool with the sissy boys and will bring them weave, bra, lipstick, panties, or whatever feminine items they want. And then we make do with what we have so like melted crayons or colored pencils make lip stick & lip liner. The net bag can be dipped in fruit punch kool aid and turned into a red fishnet tube dress. The red M & M dye can be used for lipstick and the list goes on.

INTERVIEWER: This sounds like something I definitely would NOT want to see.

FIGHT OR FUCK: It can get real freaky in here at times and now with the use of hard drugs like meth and K2 being common. Man!

INTERVIEWER: It's going down.

FIGHT OR FUCK: Hell yeah! This is another reason you don't have to take booty anymore. They give it up for drugs or while their on drugs nowadays. I keep me some cream for a freaky link. It's the perfect turn out drug.

INTERVIEWER: What is cream?

FIGHT OR FUCK: Ice, Meth, Tina, whatever you want to call it. My main boy that I sleep with now started off getting high with me then next thing you know, he started sucking my dick.

INTERVIEWER: Brought it right up out of him.

FIGHT OR FUCK: Exactly and it's too late to be ashamed when you come down. Just keep getting high, fucking & sucking, and let the time go by. You got to be really strong to not do anything strange, while you're on a strange drug, in a strange environment, alone with a stranger. The new booties don't think that far and I get in their ass every time.

INTERVIEWER: All they thinking about is getting high.

FIGHT OR FUCK: They thinking more so about getting extremely high. They don't even smoke weed no more, they smoke these strips or like this K2 and bug spray laced paper.

INTERVIEWER: Yeah I heard about that.

FIGHT OR FUCK: I keep some of that too so when they come in the room and smoke it. I just wait for them to nod out and start pulling their pants down. They can barely move so I just fuck em. They be too high to fight me off.

INTERVIEWER: Damn man! You ain't scared to catch AIDS? How much boy booty you done had in there?

FIGHT OR FUCK: Fuck AIDS! I'm already dead. I done lost count on all the booty I've had but I'd say about a hundred or maybe a little over a hundred. I kind of slowed down now though. I'm engaged.

INTERVIEWER: You got a woman on the outside?

FIGHT OR FUCK: Nall, I'm engaged to my boy CiCi. She really a girl with all that ass he got. Only time I been in love in here.

INTERVIEWER: How long you been engaged?

FIGHT OR FUCK: Every since I got that sloppy toppy, it's been love every since. I told you about the one that turned out on the meth.

INTERVIEWER: Yeah.

FIGHT OR FUCK: Yeah, he's been wanting to be someone's woman for a while and he opened all the way up to me and I fell for him. We sleep together, we shower together, we eat together, we hold hands on the yard. We do everything together.

INTERVIEWER: When you say y'all sleep together do you mean the same cell or the same bunk?

FIGHT OR FUCK: I mean the same bunk. We have a cell with two bunks but we sleep together on the bottom bunk.

INTERVIEWER: So like spooning?

FIGHT OR FUCK: Like husband and wife. We got our names tattooed on each other and nobody better not try to come between us or they gone die.

INTERVIEWER: Murder?

FIGHT OR FUCK: Bloody murder! And as the young boys say- That's on God.

LOADING

AN INTERVIEW WITH FETTY

*I*nside of the Georgia prisons that house men, the majority of the staff are female. So while these ladies get their equal employment rights, they also get the chance to live out their wildest fantasy. A chance that many of them lack the willpower to refuse once that certain bad boy gets her attention. A cougar is the primary prey of the convict seducer who's always on a mission to catch. Female officer's living double lives and having relationships with men behind bars. Do you want to know how this happens? Find out from a guy who has lipstick kisses tattooed on him to symbolize all the female prison staff that he's had intimate relations with inside the penitentiary.

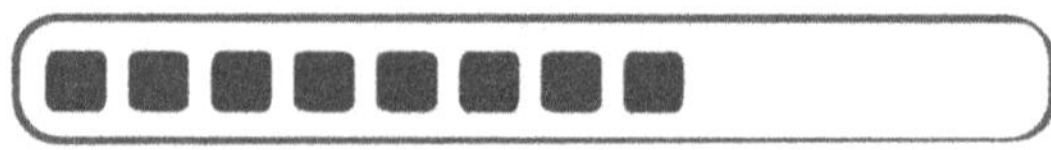

INTERVIEWER: Before we get started, can you let everyone know who you are?

FETTY: I'm human fentanyl but I go by Fetty. Everyone calls me Fetty.

INTERVIEWER: Human fentanyl damn! I hope I survive this interview *(laughing)*.

FETTY: Oh you gone be alright but ah bitch in trouble. See, I'm 100 times stronger than heroin so once she gets the slightest whiff of me she just might OD.

INTERVIEWER: That's a big statement. Where you from originally?

FETTY: I'm from East Atlanta.

INTERVIEWER: How long you been locked up?

FETTY: I been gone 13 years on a life sentence.

INTERVIEWER: Body?

FETTY: Yeah, I got two bodies from a robbery gone bad. I actually got away but they caught my codefendant and he told everything.

INTERVIEWER: Most times it's best to do dirt alone.

FETTY: Nall, I got brought in on this lick so I really shouldn't have been involved at all. I was outside my lane and got in a major accident.

INTERVIEWER: Damn! How old were you?

FETTY: 19.

INTERVIEWER: So one mistake in your teens got you sitting in prison in your 30's.

FETTY: Yep, missed all my 20's about to be 33 soon. But I accept it, two people were killed that shouldn't have. I'll make parole one day but they will never live again.

INTERVIEWER: So how you been doing your time over the years?

FETTY: At first I was fighting a lot, stabbing, getting stabbed. Just angry and on the fuckery.

INTERVIEWER: What were you doing to get into these altercations?

FETTY: Mostly taking. Robbing people for their stuff like CD players, store items, cell phones, cigarettes, drugs. Whatever I wanted or didn't have that someone else had I'd take from them. And sometimes I would have what I took but I just didn't like the person or for them to have what they had.

INTERVIEWER: What made you not like people?

FETTY: It depends like a white boy just couldn't have nothing around me for no reason other than being white. Certain dudes would make plays for contraband drops and not show love or weren't really built like that so I'd rob them.

INTERVIEWER: Were these strong arm robberies?

FETTY: To be honest, I have had a few strong arm robberies in the county jail where I just beat someone up and took their store but in prison, I did armed robbery with homemade knives.

INTERVIEWER: Did you stab first? How did the robberies go?

FETTY: I would run up in their cell with the knife out and demand what I came for. If I got any type of resistance I'd stab them. Sometimes repeatedly.

INTERVIEWER: About to catch another body.

FETTY: Yeah, I was real wild coming into the system but it came back on me a few times. I've been stabbed up by someone I robbed that caught me slipping later on. I got stabbed up by a hit man that was paid to get back at me for robbing a certain person. I've even got stabbed while trying to rob someone who happened to have a knife on them too.

INTERVIEWER: They say you live by the gun you die by the gun.

FETTY: I can go for that because one of those times was a close call for me. I almost died and had to get rushed to the hospital before I bled out. That's when I really started to re-think what I was doing and realized I wasn't the only person serving a life sentence.

Interviewer: So what did you start doing after you realized that robbing wasn't a good idea?

FETTY: Well, when you are taken out to the hospital, they have a couple of officers assigned to watch you while you're outside the prison and one of the officers was an older female who was trying to talk sense into me and asking me questions like, " Why you always in some?", " What's wrong with you?" So I told her that basically, "I didn't have nothing to lose." And from there she gave some encouraging words that led to us getting to know each other better.

INTERVIEWER: How did you all get to know each other better?

FETTY: Well, sometimes she'd work the building I was housed in so we'd talk. She might come in the dorm and kind of hang out and talk to me outside my cell or I'd talk to her at the booth. Stuff like that. Sometimes we'd be outside the building on the walk kicking it.

INTERVIEWER: Establishing a relationship in a sense?

FETTY: Yeah you can say that because it definitely became one after she started bringing me stuff.

INTERVIEWER: Stuff like what? What kind of stuff??

FETTY: I've gotten anything from weed to cell phones but first she started off feeding me like stuff from her lunch, home cooked meals, or anything I may have wanted. Once she started catching feelings, she wanted to talk to me when she got home so she brought me a phone and I would call and make sure she got home safe, talk to her late night, send the morning texts.

INTERVIEWER: The boyfriend/girlfriend routine.

FETTY: Yeah, and it was up from there. Once she brought me that phone, the dynamics of how I did my time began to change. I haven't seriously thought about robbing anyone since.

INTERVIEWER: Not even the white boys ?

FETTY: Not even them because I'd be stupid to jeopardize what I got going on.

INTERVIEWER: Right because basically you're like the man now.

FETTY: To a certain degree I was because I'm getting drops. It might not be the biggest drops but I'm getting at least a quarter pound in every week, a few phones, and I'm eating steak and shrimp on the regular. I'm making money.

INTERVIEWER: How were you getting paid?

FETTY: During this time, I was getting them to put the money on the wire, which is Western Union. Other times I'd get cash money from the guys that had it like that.

INTERVIEWER: What year was this?

FETTY: This was like 2010-11?

INTERVIEWER: Ok, the 3G era?

FETTY: Yeah, this was when people mainly had flip phones in prison and a full touch screen phone was like baller status. Data was expensive then.

INTERVIEWER: I know you had the touch screen.

FETTY: To be honest man, that's all I really had when I was messing with her. She really made sure I was straight. I really appreciate her.

INTERVIEWER: Were y'all in the same age range or was she an older lady?

FETTY: She was older but she was fine for her age. Nice shape, ass, and tittie's. She actually had a son my age though, which I believe kind of played a role in our connection.

INTERVIEWER: I can see a female having like a mother's love for someone who reminds her of her son in place like that. That's deep.

FETTY: She spoiled me and I didn't really get that from my mom coming up so I'll always remember her and the time we had together.

INTERVIEWER: So how long did the relationship last?

FETTY: We got to enjoy each other for about two years surprisingly because it wasn't a secret that we had a thing going on. And then I was fucking the hell out mom's but we lasted a good minute.

INTERVIEWER: It was like that in there?

FETTY: Yeah, we had a way we'd do things like when they had certain meals the whole dorm would go out but I'd stay back so she would come in my cell and pull her pants down half way and when I say wet. I mean she was dripping.

INTERVIEWER: How long did y'all have to do your thing?

FETTY: We'd have a good 10-15 mins before the dorm would be coming back but I didn't last over 5 minutes at first. She would be creaming and shivering as soon as I entered so I would nut instantly.

INTERVIEWER: So often did they serve these meals that everyone usually went to get?

FETTY: Once a week we'd pretty much get a chance to get intimate but she wanted to do it all the time which led to our relationship ending.

INTERVIEWER: Damn! What happened?

FETTY: So she kind of started free styling and coming in the room too frequently with the wrong inmates noticing it so someone wrote a kite(note) to the warden about it and I got transferred on accusations of personal dealings with staff.

INTERVIEWER: That sucks!

FETTY: Man, I was so mad and I stayed in the hole for 30 days before they transferred me. But it also made me realize that I can't get lost in the sauce. I gotta always remember that I'm locked up and nothing lasts forever.

INTERVIEWER: So you get to next prison and it's back to the basics.

FETTY: As it pertains to having a woman inside the prison, I had to start over but I had a lot of free world items that indicated that I wasn't the average inmate. Then I had cash money and money saved on the outside so I was in position to make moves and eventually catch again.

INTERVIEWER: What kind of free world items did you have?

FETTY: I had like Cartier glasses, gold diamond necklace, gold diamond ring, a couple of G-Shock watches, designer underwear, socks, t-shirts. I had Air Jordan tennis shoes and slides. My baby spoiled me so I had a lot of stuff dudes didn't have. I even had real cologne disguised in eye-drop bottles and mixed in my lotion. Then I kept a clean pressed state uniform, a clean cut, and a clean shave with a neat mustache on top of all that.

INTERVIEWER: Ok, you were like prison GQ?

FETTY: Most Definitely.

INTERVIEWER: Did you maintain contact with your lady from the last prison?

FETTY: I still talk to her til this day and she keeps money on my books but I still have to campaign where I'm at. She can decide to move on at any moment and I will have to respect it. I don't put it in her face but what's understood don't need to be explained.

INTERVIEWER: So how did it go once you got to the next prison?

FETTY: It was hard on me sexually. Sexual frustration was at an all-time high for me and I retired from jacking my dick after I started getting pussy in prison. I told myself that I ain't shit if I can't get a country girl to like me.

INTERVIEWER: No porn on the phone or nothing?

FETTY: None of that and I think it helped me catch faster because for some reason, it seemed like females were attract-ed to me more when I hadn't released in over a month. The females would just start talking to me.

INTERVIEWER: I heard something like this on YouTube with a guy talking about semen retention and NOFAP.

FETTY: It's real man I think it's tied to reproduction with the opposite sex and with the majority of guys in prison jacking, I think it made me stand out more to the females.

INTERVIEWER: So you're clean cut, got the Cartier frames on, and you're on semen retention. What happened next?

FETTY: I caught another cougar.

INTERVIEWER: You and these cougars

FETTY: Yeah man I caught another one but at this camp it was a trend for the female officers to have an inmate boyfriend. This camp was a bit more live than the last camp.

INTERVIEWER: So how did this relationship come about?

FETTY: She was choosing on me man, as soon as I got there. She would always be looking at me, she'd speak, ask about my glasses. Stuff like that so we'd kick it a little bit. I showed her my photo album and stuff but I saw that I really had her when I noticed her watching me every time I'd workout. So I decided to get her to desire me more by doing a little trick l learned from one of my OG convict buddies. We'll call this "the sausage".

INTERVIEWER: The sausage?

FETTY: Yeah, because that's mainly what a cougar wants from a young man. That's what's on her mind, it's her desire to get some young dick. So what I'd do is I'd have someone make me like a jock strap and I'll put one of those hot summer sausage's in the jock strap pouch, put the jock strap on, and go workout in my grey shorts.

INTERVIEWER: What the hell?

FETTY: It's the perfect mind fuck for a female that's watching you work out and that sausage is just swinging in them grey shorts while you do jumping jacks or she can see the print while you're doing sit ups and pull ups. Combine this, with her already liking you, she gone be mesmerized with a wet pussy and ready to take a chance with you.

INTERVIEWER: I can only imagine.

FETTY: And from there, everything just fell in place because before she went home that day, she made it her business to ask me if I need her to do anything for me.

INTERVIEWER: And the saga continues?

FETTY: I'm back on line with a cell phone the next day, I'm getting drops again, I'm fucking. I'm back to my old self within 4 months. But like I said, this camp was more live so the officers wanted to like be seen with their man and they watched each other back while they fucked and made drops the whole nine.

INTERVIEWER: Give some examples of what you mean.

FETTY: Ok, like when they ran chow or fed the dorm, the officers would stand outside their respective buildings to monitor the inmates on the walk going to the dining hall but at the same time the inmate boyfriends would be posted up outside with their girl or whatever for the officer to like show off her man to the other female officer that's working another building. A cougar gets like extra points if her boyfriend is someone fly that the young female officer's will want. It was like a showcase and soap opera mixed together.

INTERVIEWER: And you said they would watch each other's back?

FETTY: Yeah, so they had crews or certain officers that messed with each other and knew each other business that would signal when things were clear for them to go ahead and fuck on their man and kind of like make sure no one caught them. They would deliver packages or hold packages for each other if it was hot in a certain dorm. It was a team effort that was a gift and a curse.

INTERVIEWER: How was it a gift and a curse?

FETTY: Well, this is how jealousy and love triangles start also because one might tell the other how good she got fucked, now the other one want some. Or one might feel like the other one got a better man. Or one is just attracted to and is crushing on the other ones man so she be trying little slick stuff. All the various female things.

INTERVIEWER: Did anything in particular happened involving a friend of your cougar?

Fetty: Yeah, so I was a night orderly who would stay out at night to clean up while the rest of the dorm had to lock down. It was a room inside the dorm that had like a desk and some chairs in it that was reserved for the counselor whenever they came to the building. Me and my lady used to have some good fuck sessions at night in this room. It was a younger female officer that worked with her that would be our look out and she had her something going on with a dude too, but she wanted to get with me. So one night, my lady didn't come to work but had a package for me that she sent through the younger female officer. When the young officer gives me the package, she say, "You let her taste it when you gone let me taste it?"

INTERVIEWER: Whaattttt!

FETTY: I was caught off guard so I was speechless at first but then I told her to stop playing until she licked her lips and told me she didn't play. Long story short, she gave me some of the best head that night and my first love triangle was formed.

INTERVIEWER: This sounds like trouble but I meant to ask you how were they getting past the metal detector with the phones and stuff?

FETTY: The metal detector only picked up on the battery so what I had my ladies to do was take the batteries out the phones and wrap them in black electrical tap. Depending on her size, she would either strap the contraband on her body or put stuff under her tittie's. And sometimes, they were working together so whoever was over the metal detector would just let them walk through. It just depends.

INTERVIEWER: How did you deal with the haters because I know they were present?

FETTY: Anytime it's a female involved, it's gone be a male hater but I will say, at this camp, the guys were convicts so they didn't do no police stuff but they would try to push up and black mail my lady, threaten her and talk down on me and stuff so I'd have to go check dudes and even put hands on dudes about approaching or disrespecting my lady. Not very often but it happened a few times.

INTERVIEWER: So getting back to this love triangle, I know you had some situations with that?

FETTY: Yeah, it got crazy with the young girl because she was trying to do the most man. She wanted to take pics and make porno flicks. It got wild and it was my fault too because I was down with the drama filled adventure.

INTERVIEWER: So y'all took pictures and made videos together inside the prison?

FETTY: Yeah, I got some exclusive footage saved on my drive. We got homemade prison porn where I got her handcuffed beating that thang up.

INTERVIEWER: Stop lying. I know she ain't let you do all that now.

FETTY: Officer uniform on, hands cuffed behind her back, bent over, pants down, recorded. I wouldn't lie to you and we got like couple pictures kissing, hugged up. I got the prison uniform on and she got the officer uniform on. No cap.

INTERVIEWER: Wow man! I would've never thought nothing like this goes on.

FETTY: And she wasn't no ugly or no fat girl.

INTERVIEWER: I was just about to ask that.

FETTY: Yeah, she was nice. It just gets real once the feelings involved and on top of that she competing with my cougar so she trying to have one up on her so she going extra hard.

INTERVIEWER: I can see that being her logic but how was your cougar acting?

FETTY: My cougar wasn't really aware of what all we had going on so she was chilling. It just all hit the fan when the young girl got pregnant and she didn't want nobody else messing with me. She got real emotional during the pregnancy.

INTERVIEWER: She got pregnant? Aww man!

FETTY: Yeah, she kept the baby too and raised pure hell beforehand. She actually had a fist fight with my cougar telling her how she was pregnant with my baby and my cougar was trying to mess up our family when she got her own family and marriage to attend to at home. It got messy bro. Real chain gang soap opera.

INTERVIEWER: Damn! So the cougar was married?

FETTY: Yeah, her husband worked at the prison as the food service director.

INTERVIEWER: She was playing it raw. Sheesh!

FETTY: She say he was cheating so according to her, they both were living double lives.

INTERVIEWER: It's a dirty game out here!

FETTY: Indeed. I just play my part, you know.

INTERVIEWER: Right. So now that you're a father, the young girl has like maneuvered a permanent position in your life?

FETTY: It's crazy because when I look back on it, she was playing for keeps the whole time. I was just enjoying the moment but it's cool she added to my life and I love her for that.

INTERVIEWER: So if they let you out tomorrow that's who you going home to?

FETTY: Definitely. This my bitch, like the cougars, was more so just having fun with me but the young girl has her heart and soul involved. Like she gone move wherever I go. If they transfer me, she gone try to get a job there, like she doing any and everything to stay with me.

INTERVIEWER: Ok, she your ride or die. That's dope.

FETTY: Yeah, she'll help me escape if I wanted her to, but I'm not quite ready to pull that stunt yet.

INTERVIEWER: Escaping is the easy part I hear but living on the run is hard.

FETTY: That's why I said I'm not ready yet. You really need some money, a new identity, and a foreign destination that doesn't extradite in order to successfully escape in my opinion.

INTERVIEWER: Sounds about right. Anything else you want say?

FETTY: Although I've had my wild experiences inside of prison, it doesn't compare to the experiences I can have as a free man. The female officer's come to work and have their fun but go home to freedom every day while I still have to reside in bondage. Freedom trumps anything you can get imprisoned.

INTERVIEWER: Word.

LOADING

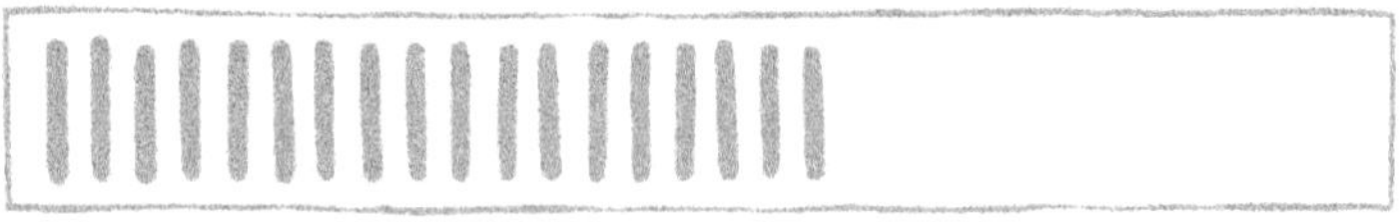

AN INTERVIEW WITH SLICK

*I*n this interview, you gotta pay close attention because the message is conveyed in a slick manner with a lot of news you can use. This guy really lives by his name and really Plays the Game. You'll never hear another prison romance story quite like this one.

INTERVIEWER: What's going on Slick man! I want to start off first by asking how did you get your name?

SLICK: My peers named me that in the 5th grade and it stuck with me throughout my life. I actually live up to my name in the present but not by being slimy or nothing like that.

INTERVIEWER: What kind of things were you into before going to prison?

SLICK: so before When I came to prison, I was a young fly dude just really getting my feet wet you know, in the Game, I had a couple of PimP mentors lacing me, I was pursuing a rap career, I had a little money, my own house, and a couple of cars. I was doing really good for my age.

INTERVIEWER: What was your rap name?

SLICK: I started off as Playher Slayher, then I changed my name to DA$, then D.A., and finally Sport'n Slick.

INTERVIEWER: Why so many name changes?

SLICK: Well, my first name could be misconstrued as me wanting to slay the Players so I changed that immediately to DA$ which stood for "Dead Ass Serious" with the dollar sign to symbolize being serious about the money. I took the S off because I didn't want to be confused with Daz Dillinger. After I came home from prison, I released the old music as Sport'n Slick.

INTERVIEWER: So you got music out on streaming platforms?

SLICK: Yeah, I have two singles out on all platforms "Outcha Ass" and "Get Get." I don't really promote it because I'm no longer serious about being a rapper but I do believe in finishing anything I start. So you can definitely stream it if you're into hardcore PimP tunes. These songs were made in the rockstar era and produced by Don P of Trillville, so it's kind of like crunk music. K.Y recorded and mixed the songs.

I don't know if you heard of K.Y but he is a legendary mix engineer these days.

INTERVIEWER: Ok, I'ma check that out. So you had real production on these songs and went to prison in midst of everything?

SLICK: I had a mix tape that I worked with DJ Smooth to make that was going to create a buzz leading up to the new singles. I literally had an appointment to take the singles to get mastered by Glenn, another legend, and pick up 1,000 copies of the mix tape on the day they revoked my bond. And after that I didn't see the streets again for eleven years.

INTERVIEWER: That's crazy bro and how old were you when you went in?

SLICK: I was 22 years old man.

INTERVIEWER: How much time did you get?

SLICK: I lost at trial and received 20 years.

Interviewer: Dayyum.

Slick: So when I came into the prison system, it was my first time and you know my main objective once I got my time, you know, trying to figure out how to get out I'm wanting to get out of prison. I want to get my freedom back. You know, having 20 years at 22 years old, was like you know basically being sentenced to do my life all over again as an inmate.

INTERVIEWER: That's heavy!

SLICK: So, you know, when I was out, I had a lot of different females that was infatuated with me because of my positioning and who I was. And you know, the Player in me just wouldn't allow me to entertain emotional connections and things of that nature. I wasn't really trying to get emotionally connected with females, even though you know, they might write letters and stuff like that. My position was always, "where is the money" you know? How you trying to help me get out of prison, how this gonna help me get back out?

INTERVIEWER: Real stiff like.

SLICK: Yeah, I wasn't trying to entertain any relationship or emotional type stuff with females in the beginning of my bid. I like always brushed them off because I had my own money still. I was putting my own money on my books, buying my own packages, so I basically was able to take care of myself. I'll say roughly, you know, between me, and the assistance that my mom would give me on her own, made it where for the first four years of my sentence. I was pretty much self-sufficient.

INTERVIEWER: As far as basic prison expenses?

SLICK: Right. I was able to take care of that now as far as being able to pay lawyers and the extracurricular prison stuff like phones and drugs. I didn't really have it to do all of that. I didn't have a substantial amount of money to pay for that. So you know I'm doing a lot of fighting on my case by myself and later on in my bid, I eventually started running out of money. I didn't have the movement. I could've or should've had because I was green to a lot of stuff so I wasn't making no money I was just spending my money. So it took me about four years for my money to get to a point where I'm like," what I'm gone do."

INTERVIEWER: You gotta figure something out when that money get funny?

SLICK: For real and I didn't want to put no pressure on my mom so I started to compromise a little bit as far as my position on not getting emotionally attached to no female out there because I mean, to be honest, I wasn't trusting a woman like to be faithful out there on the street. And then on top of that, you know, I'm a Player, and it's PimPing with me so I want some money.

INTERVIEWER: Right right right!

SLICK: So in 2011, I got back in touch with this female who was actually married to some dude when I was out but they were going through what they were going through in the marriage so she wanted to use me as like a side dude that she can cheat with or someone to rebound to. But I wasn't with it because like I say, I was trying to get some money. I was try- ing to send her out the door so we weren't on the same page.

INTERVIEWER: So you never had sex with her?

SLICK: No, I didn't. She gave me a little sample of head but I never penetrated her. I believe that's what kept her infatuat- ed over the years because she was an attractive female.

INTERVIEWER: Yeah, she probably wasn't used to being turned down when it came to sex.

SLICK: Right. And over the years, that I'd been locked up, she finally divorced the dude, started back dating and got dragged through the mud, so now when I talk back to her, she wants to help me get out and be there for me while I'm in prison. At least this is how she talking. So we started talking and I'm seeing this as an opportunity where you know, worst case scenario, I can have someone to help me out financially during this time where I'm really running out of money. So in the process, she tells me that she has a pending charge herself.

INTERVIEWER: It's always a catch.

SLICK: Ain't it man. So she's asking me what she need to do because she don't really understand the law. She want my insight as to what they can do to her and how she can get out of it.

INTERVIEWER: Oh! She getting her some free legal advice from a seasoned convict.

SLICK: Their always looking for guidance when it's hard times so I look her case up for her and gave her some information to take to her attorney to make sure she didn't get a raw deal. Long story short, she pled out to a misdemeanor after being charged with a felony. But I remember like prior to this, I had talked to her before, say like two years prior and she sent me a couple of things but prior to her reaching what I perceived as her low point, she wasn't really serious about seeing about me behind the wall. It wasn't just her but you'll talk to them and they'll say, "oh! I'ma come see you," "how I get on the visitation list," blah blah blah, but then they don't follow through. They may even get on your list, like she did, but they don't never show. They always say they want to see you but then they don't show up. It's just something that females be thinking they should say to a guy that they know who is locked up. But as life goes on, out of sight-out of mind kicks in, and all that enthusiasm about coming to see you is short lived especially when it's not right around the corner. They got to come, they got to travel because most prisons be way outside the city limits. So they got to travel to come see you. So all that talk be short lived.

INTERVIEWER: Until….

SLICK: That low point.

INTERVIEWER: Mmmm hmm!

SLICK: She facing charges, she getting ran through by these dudes, nobody trying to get married. So you know, she computes the time and then at this time, you know I'm supposed to be coming up for parole in. Like two years where it wasn't guaranteed that I was gonna make it, but it was highly probable that I was. So when she see that and then on top of that she got two kids so in her mind, riding with me for two years and sort of getting a break from the streets. You know, showing herself as being down for me or whatever, will put her in position to work on herself and have a good man at home in two years who is also somebody she been wanted to get with anyway.

INTERVIEWER: She rode when it made sense for her to ride.

SLICK: If you know, you know, but I ain't mad because on my end, I'm looking at it like even though I'm not wanting to be in a relationship or whatever, but right now it's in my best interest to you lock in and get some support from the outside. So I gotta you know kind of compromise on how I want to move and you know, try to play a square relationship role and if she so happens to do the unbelievable and ride out for X amount of years without cheating and doing everything, I need her to do while I'm inside the prison. Then she will actually deserve the compromise I been giving. I'd actually mess with her and live the married life with her on the outside.

INTERVIEWER: From Pimpin to simpin.

SLICK: Although I've been laced with Game, I never did any Pimpin per se, although some people may say that I have, and I wasn't doing no simpin either. I simply played my hand sir.

INTERVIEWER: My apologies Mr. Slick. I'd never want to offend a Game Member.

SLICK: No offense taken. I just had to set the record straight but moving along.

INTERVIEWER: Yeah, so what happened next?

SLICK: So she finally comes to see me at the prison where we sit in an open area for contact visits. And this is how I knew she was at one of her lows. She comes in looking good, a lot of the guys used to give me props because I really got the baddest chick coming up to visitation. And the officers monitoring visitation really didn't care, so I got a chance to get a little frisky

INTERVIEWER: Fucking in visitation?

SLICK: Nall, I fingered her but don't get me wrong, it does happen.

INTERVIEWER: Ok, so you're up there getting the stink finger.

SLICK: Yeah, but this stink was offensive, like strong fishy stink. It was an embarrassing stink up the whole room type of scent.

INTERVIEWER: Head jerk?

SLICK: That was the automatic response when I put my finger within proximity of my nose.

INTERVIEWER: Don't tell me the other visitors smelled it...

SLICK: Yeah man! So you know the other female visitors making faces and comments. It was embarrassing.

INTERVIEWER: So your girl come in looking fine with a stinking behind?

SLICK: It was terrible but that let me know the quality of dudes she'd been dealing with and that she hadn't been properly caring for herself, but this is our first time seeing each other and we aren't in a relationship yet, so I'm still trying to turn this situation into some Pimping. So when we would talk she'd be on the fence about it with questions like, "How can I guide and protect her as a turn out when she goes out if I'm in prison?" you know that sort of thing so I asked her about the dudes she was talking to and basically encouraged her to get the money that I need for the lawyer out of the dudes she was already dating.

INTERVIEWER: Oh word?

SLICK: Yeah, so she tells me about this white guy who liked her and was trying to fly her out to California to hang out so I told her to tell him to send her the money for the trip which she did and he sent it. However, she got cold feet and didn't want to go, so I called him from prison as if I was home and told him I saw the messages and that he needed to stop contacting my lady. He apologized and texted her saying that he wanted her to donate the money he sent to the humane society. But she did not.

INTERVIEWER: We know where that money went *(laughing)*.

Slick: As the late Pimp C once said, "Commissary is very necessary." So I appreciated his donation.

INTERVIEWER: So at what point did y'all seriously become a couple?

SLICK: I tried my hand at flipping her for a little while but it was hard to do from prison especially when she really wants to be in a square relationship. So the conversations would be about how she's saving money for a lawyer without turning tricks and we can get money other ways and she's going to do this and do that and that. She just wants to be a wife. At this time I'm down to my last $700 and her conversation gave me a pretty much guaranteed way to lock her and make dividends off my last $700. I called my mom and tell her to find me a nice wedding and engagement ring set with my last money. She questioned my logic at first but later found a great deal on a set at the pawn shop, took pictures, and sent them to my phone. After I saw the ring and confirmed for my mom to purchase it, I just let everything flow organically from us talking every day, me sending poems, drawings, and her coming to visit one to two times each month. I finally popped the question around tax time after us dating for about 4 months.

INTERVIEWER: Killed the PimPin damn?

SLICK: Nall, I just played dead.

INTERVIEWER: You did wait until tax time though.

(Both burst into laughter).

SLICK: Timing is everything you know.

INTERVIEWER: Facts. So how did the whole proposal with the engagement ring go?

SLICK: Well, I told her that I had a gift for her to pick up from my mom, so she goes to meet my mom and is surprised with the white gold and diamond ring which happened to be of higher quality than any of the jewelry she had at the time. She was so happy and then to seal the deal, the very next time that she came to visit, I got on one knee in the visitation room and asked if she would she marry me.

INTERVIEWER: Lock game vicious.

SLICK: But at the same time, I felt like such a lame on the inside for getting down on one knee.

INTERVIEWER: A man's gotta do what a man's gotta do, not so?

SLICK: I knew that's what she wanted so I went ahead with it to get what I needed from the situation. She rode with me for a little over a year traveling from prison to prison (I got transferred twice within that time period from North Georgia to South Georgia) and then we got legally married at the prison which was the official lock for her to feel secure in knowing she's going to have the man she wants after doing whatever amount of time she has to do with me. However, she forgot to bring my wedding band which was rather ironic.

INTERVIEWER: Oh wow! So how does the prison marriage work? Do you get a tuxedo to wear?

SLICK: No. So I had to wear my state prison uniform and what they do is have the prison chaplain as the officiant and we have like a short visitation where we exchange vows and eat a few snacks afterwards, then it's over.

INTERVIEWER: Ok so what did she get to wear?

SLICK: The attire is pretty much the same as for visitation but she came in and showed out with this tight black dress and stilletos with her booty on hydraulics. Yeah, she showed out up there for the wedding I must say. I don't think they would have let her in if it was a normal visit.

INTERVIEWER: From the sound of things, you really didn't go out bad!

SLICK: Depending on how you look at it you're right. It was a double edged investment where I utilized my last money to get someone else to spend that same money ten times back on me because to be honest, I wasn't going to do nothing but put the money on my books. Then I was taking the pressure off my mom to have to send me anything for the next few years and secured myself a residence upon release because I really didn't want to have to move back in with my mom, you know.

INTERVIEWER: Right, it was a lot of benefits to this move.

SLICK: It had to be in order for me to make that compromise because I was biased against being a stepdad and I didn't really want to be in a square relationship. My mindset wasn't on falling in love and having a wife and all that I just want some money.

INTERVIEWER: So you're married now. How did things change?

SLICK: I really feel like she was going harder for me before the marriage but I think she got more comfortable afterwards. She wasn't no ugly or fat girl, she was chocolate, thick, with a fat ass so when she came to visitation, she is in the top 5% appearance wise so the officers and other inmates would always salute me for having a bad wife in there. I done even had officers who would straight up hate with comments like why she married to this guy locked up and she can do better etc.

INTERVIEWER: And these people go home every day... that's crazy.

SLICK: I literally have haters everywhere I go. It was this one lieutenant I had to check about getting out of bounds with the comments to my lady when I went back to the county jail for court one time.

INTERVIEWER: You got to think though, if a person thinks you are beneath them because you're locked up and you got a better woman than them, that will make them feel insecure and jealous, so it's a compliment really.

SLICK: Yeah, and I think these compliments kind of went to her head over time.

INTERVIEWER: How was the intimacy leading up to the marriage?

SLICK: Well, before and after the visits, we were able to hug and kiss for a few minutes so that was one way. And then I either had my own cellphone or was on contract to rent someone else's, so we were able to have phone sex regularly.

INTERVIEWER: You don't seem like you'd be into that.

SLICK: Well, I actually wasn't and had never done it until I started messing her. She's actually the only person I ever had phone sex with.

INTERVIEWER: Damn! She turned you out all type of ways.

SLICK: She did that I can't even lie like she's the one that introduced me to it and kind of showed me the ropes which wasn't a bad experience for a convict. It was a lot of guys fucking boys and pulling they dick out on officers but I wasn't one of them.

INTERVIEWER: Salute.

SLICK: And then I realized some things about women and how they have different fetishes. See she was like a cum freak, something I wouldn't have known if we didn't start having phone sex. I'm not going to go in detail but this is what led up to her asking me for cum videos and pics.

INTERVIEWER: Oh y'all was getting nasty?

SLICK: Yeah, to say the least and man, it's crazy because I actually got caught having phone sex with her by one of the CERT Team officers.

INTERVIEWER: Naughty, naughty.

SLICK: Right. That was too embarrassing and I lost my phone.

INTERVIEWER: What's a CERT officer? And how did he catch you slipping like that?

SLICK: So a CERT officer is an officer that is on the CERT team which is like a prison task force. They do all the shakedowns and ass whooping of inmates similar to the police on the street that do drug raids and apprehend people with violent arrest warrants.

INTERVIEWER: Ok.

SLICK: So this particular day, we were having cheese burger and potato wedges, so everyone went to the dining hall except a few people. I paid someone to bring me the meal back so I could have the phone sex session but unbeknownst to everyone, the CERT Team had an unconventional raid planned for our dorm at a time that they usually would have been gone home. So instead of the guys coming back to the dorm from the dining hall, they were all escorted to the gym to be searched and held in there until the CERT Team finished shaking down the dorm. The CERT officer that caught me was coming to get anyone who was still in the dorm and have them go to the gym. No one was in the dorm as a look-out so I didn't know the officer was in there which led came to him unlocking the cell door and catching me with my dick in my hand.

INTERVIEWER: Geee whizzz! *(laughing).*

SLICK: And during this time, we were only able to be intimate with each other over the phone because they had taken her off my visitation list.

INTERVIEWER: Why? What happened?

SLICK: As a matter of fact, this kind of pushed the marriage more towards priority because when I first put her on my visitation list, I put her on as my cousin at a certain camp. Because you know, they were approving all family members, they didn't have to be immediate just any family member and they would just approve them with no verification. So before I even thought about being in a relationship with her, she was on my visitation list as my cousin. So when the chief counselor, another hater, was working visitation one weekend, he saw us kissing so he decided the following week to put out a memo requiring the inmate population to update their visitation list to verify all extended family members.

INTERVIEWER: When you say verify, does that mean like they had to pass a background check or something?

SLICK: Correct. Anybody who is not immediate family was limited to two people and they had to pass a background check.

INTERVIEWER: Ok gotcha.

SLICK: And so this time she changed her relationship status from cousin to fiancée and that's when we ran into a problem where she wasn't able to come to visitation for about a good six months. Initially, because they said she put false information when coming to visitation, but I filed a grievance saying that was a personal bias because in Georgia, it's not against the law to marry your cousin even though she wasn't my cousin, we stuck to that so they couldn't justify taking her off my list for lying.

INTERVIEWER: Alright Johnny Cochran. I see you.

SLICK: The gift of gab is interchangeable but they still denied her because she was on probation, saying that she wouldn't be allowed to go on my list until she was off probation. Even though she didn't have too much longer on probation, the marriage guaranteed her getting back on my list because she would be considered immediate family.

INTERVIEWER: So once y'all got married, they put her back on?

SLICK: Actually, they didn't because they wanted me to provide proof of the marriage license and all that but before that was done, I got transferred to another prison.

INTERVIEWER: Ok, so you get to the new prison....

SLICK: So I get to the next prison and at this time I had a bunch of grievances about the visitation and other stuff against the chief counselor dude, so when I get to go to camp, that's when they finally you know, put her back on my list once I show the proof of marriage. And I'll never forget the Deputy Warden who added her back asking me, "Why y'all want to get married now? Why y'all didn't just remain friends and then she just help you out or be here for you as a friend until you get out and then once you get out and are able to see everything that's going on then if y'all think it's good for y'all to get married then get married then."

INTERVIEWER: That was logical but you Playing

SLICK: Right. But I ain't wanna say that, so I really didn't have a response other than we just wanted to do it now so this is when she dropped the play on me. She was like, "I don't know, she's using you for something because I just don't see a woman that is out there free wanting to marry a man who is locked up. If it's not something she is getting out of it, I just want to tell you she using you for something."

INTERVIEWER: Damn! Auntie done hated! Was this an older lady?

SLICK: Yeah, she was in my mom's age range and she always looked out for me when she could. But in hindsight and as I look back on the situation, she was really just telling the truth in case I was totally green about female nature. It's just like what Mike Tyson said about how you can't expect to find a woman to love you the way your mother does because, " A woman loves you for her survival and your mother loves you for your survival."

INTERVIEWER: Yeah, Mike Tyson dropped bars with that and auntie been told you that just in another way?

SLICK: Right. So when you look at it like when she came to me, she was kind of like ran through, you know. She was getting dragged by various different guys like they wasn't trying to be or, they wasn't trying to stay with her over a year or whatever. And so she was basically, you know, to being in relationships having sex with these guys doing this, that, and the third but at the end of the day, all she was getting was fucked. Wasn't nobody coming and trying to be no stepdad. They weren't trying to get married, they weren't trying to do all that. Then she catches a charge so now she's facing time, you know, she really ain't got her shit together like that. So coming to me incarcerated. It was like her love for me, even though it was something for me to get out of it. She was really saving herself, because you know, her focusing on me was making it where she took a break from, you know, the pattern of conduct she was having that wasn't getting her nowhere out there. She was able to get help from somebody who's going through the same shit like once she caught a charge to give her some comfort and direction on what she need to do and then on top of that, she actually had a crush on me from when I was on street, so she already see the potential, and what type of man I am. And not to mention, she has two boys with absentee fathers. So I'm a good candidate to be an example for her boys that need to become men.

INTERVIEWER: And she got the coveted wedding ring from the situation.

SLICK: You know, she actually was using me for something. She was using me to save herself and a lot of things, believe it or not, from what type of car she was in, what type of things she was into doing, and like how she evolved as a woman.

And you know, she was able to get you know her credit and stuff together, her ambition, her confidence and stuff from messing with me throughout that time, she actually grew and became a homeowner and all type of stuff during the time that she was messing with me as opposed to prior, she wasn't really flourishing like that so she did have a use for me.

INTERVIEWER: So basically she wasn't shit until she got with Slick.

SLICK: All you have to do is check the Carfax. And once she got that better positioning and I was still imprisoned and kept getting set off by the parole board. You know, that's when things started to kind of turn for the worse where I began to get the impression that I didn't really need to stay in the marriage.

INTERVIEWER: Damn! The honeymoon is over. How long were y'all married when you started thinking about divorce?

SLICK: We were married about 18 months before I started really having second thoughts because we'd kind of fall out about certain etiquettes and her feeling the need to go out a lot. But we didn't have a big fall out until later on which I'll get to after I finish telling this part.

INTERVIEWER: ok, that's fine.

SLICK: So I get to the next camp where she is added back to my visitation and we're now able to get our hug's and feels again. I'm also hustling a lot more with the cigarettes, weed, and selling phone time. So she was able to help me in managing the accounts for the funds I was accumulating. During this time, I was able to get my credit and bank account set up so I got in position as well during the relationship. As I intended anyway, because it was a long shot to me for her to be able to uphold or be able to stay down like she said she would. Especially after the two years when they were supposed to had let me out, but instead, they set me off for another three more years and some change to make me have to serve an even ten years of the twenty.

INTERVIEWER: Damn! Why did they do that?

SLICK: No reason, because I hadn't been in trouble or anything they just be wanting certain guys to do more time so in my case they said it would be incompatible with the welfare of society for me to be released at that time with no further explanation.

INTERVIEWER: Wow!

SLICK: So now the time that she was expecting me to come home I wasn't coming home, so things started to kind of change after that. I mean, she stayed coming through for me but I could just tell.

INTERVIEWER: The vibe was different.

SLICK: Right the little nuances that can't be concealed but she stayed. She stuck around and I wound up getting transferred to a county prison the following year which is like a work camp where everyone pretty much goes outside in the free world during the week to do free prison labor for the county.

INTERVIEWER: I've thrown a few packs of cigarettes and things out my car window for those guys. I be seeing them cutting grass and stuff so I know what you're talking about.

SLICK: Right, that's real. So when I get to the county camp, I'm getting drops and my lady and I were finally able to actually have sex.

INTERVIEWER: I can go for that. How did y'all make it happen?

SLICK: So at first we were sneaky with it but my detail officer was cool so he let his workers smoke and have phones on the truck we just couldn't leave anything on the truck.

INTERVIEWER: Shout out to the detail officer.

SLICK: Yeah, he was a real one and we'd go to the same spots to have our one hour lunch break, so the first spot was a park inside of a neighborhood that had a bathroom. And what I did was I got the address, sent it to my lady, and when she was off work during the week, she would come down there around lunchtime and beat us to the park but park her car, like it was at one of the houses, then go in the bathroom with Lysol, bleach, wipes, rags, and a blanket until we got there. So when we pull up to the park, it looks empty and the detail officer let us off the truck to eat and use the restroom or whatever and from there I'd go in the bathroom and get straight to the business.

INTERVIEWER: Ok now I'm starting to see why they call you Slick.

SLICK: We done fucked in her car while it was parked in the woods. It was unreal like all those desires, long thoughts, and visualizations we had of being able to sneak in one of those closets or bathrooms at visitation over the years manifested on that detail. Man, I could've escaped if we were on that.

INTERVIEWER: Detail officer rocking with you.

SLICK: He was so cool that one time. She was down there but we was on a job site that we couldn't leave from that day so I told him just to see if he would take us to the park real quick, but he was like just have her come on the truck.

INTERVIEWER: You lying.

SLICK: Bro on God! We fucked on the back of the truck with them weed eaters and chainsaws.

INTERVIEWER: Hell nall! *(Bursts into laughter)*.

SLICK: I can't make this up. I was having my way on that detail. I'm talking about eating how I want to and I had someone suit casing my weed back into the facility.

INTERVIEWER: Suit case?

SLICK: Let me explain. So I had someone to stuff my marijuana up there ass so that it would be able to get back into the county prison because they strip searched us every time we came back in from detail. So the rectum is called a Louis Bag or a suitcase and when someone transports items through their rectum, that's called "suitcasing."

INTERVIEWER: Boy, y'all got a helluva lingo in there and I bet that was some stanking weed- I mean the real loud pack!

SLICK: Now, sometimes the weed would get shitty but that's when whoever was suitcasing didn't properly wrap it before making the deposit. I didn't experience that personally because I had a veteran suitcaser and my reign at the county prison was short lived anyway.

INTERVIEWER: Noooo!

SLICK: Yeah man, I had to turn the P into a G.

INTERVIEWER: What that mean?

SLICK: I went from being a Player to being a gangster or a gorilla which is a problem I have when it comes to Playing myself out of position. I don't violate people, so my pride and ego, when someone violates me can be overwhelming at times. I had a little under a pound of weed stashed outside and one of the guys on the truck had the nerve to steal it when I didn't go out to detail one day.

INTERVIEWER: How did you find out who actually got it?

SLICK: I just did deductive reasoning and selected the person I believe got it.

INTERVIEWER: So it's a possibility that they didn't even get it?

Slick: Possibly, but the likelihood is so small that if they didn't get it, they were just due for a bad day.

Interviewer: Damn! So what happened?

SLICK: I locked a padlock onto a belt loop and wrapped the other end of the belt around my hand and beat the guy across the head with the lock several times.

INTERVIEWER: So you split the guys head open with a lock man?

SLICK: Yeah, he had to go to the hospital and get stitches. They booked and fingerprinted me with a new charge; they raised my security, put me in the hole for like 70 days, and then transferred me to a one of the most violent prisons in the state.

INTERVIEWER: How did the wife react?

SLICK: Oh, she was highly upset, saying I jeopardized everything from us having our fun on detail to being able to make parole on time.

INTERVIEWER: You did that now.

SLICK: You're right. Regardless of my rationale for doing it, the marriage went more and more downhill because now once I get to the other camp, it's like resentment because she feel like now it's my fault I'm at this camp. And I made our relationship more difficult because of the decision I made to do what I did to dude about something that could have really been replaced. So now she wants to act out too, all of a sudden wanting to wear more provocative clothing when she goes out just stuff. I wasn't feeling, so long story short I filed for divorce.

INTERVIEWER: Clearly, you will say fuck that shit!

SLICK: I felt like divorce was necessary because her unspoken words were saying that she wanted to be free because with her doing all that 9 times out of 10 it's going to lead to something else so I don't need, because I'm big on my reputation and I got homeboys, family, and other people that be seeing her and know this is my wife. So the last thing I want to hear is that they saw my wife doing such and such or this or that dude fucking on my wife. I ain't really trying to hear that or more importantly have my honor tainted because I'm married to this female when she showing me she out there trying to do her own thing.

INTERVIEWER: Yeah, because I could have sworn you were supposed to be some type of player or something.

SLICK: Exactly so. Before I let her Play me like an entire sucker, let me take this marriage jacket off and come to the realization that I pretty much got what I needed out the situation to the point where I'm really self-sufficient now. And if she was to leave, I would be able to take care of myself until I got out and worst case scenario, get another female or whatever. But it was a simple process getting the divorce since I filed it in this little country town where the prison was located.

INTERVIEWER: How long did it take to get the divorce finalized?

SLICK: It took them about six to eight months to finalize the divorce of our three year marriage.

INTERVIEWER: How did it go afterwards? Did y'all stop messing with each other?

SLICK: Nall, she stuck around a little for about a year. I mean, we still was together but we just wasn't married because my thing was based on the way she was moving. She wasn't ready to be married. So I ask her like, "Why should

I be in here married to you and you running around out there like you ain't married? I can wait. I ain't got no problem with being with you, I just ain't gone be married to you right now."

INTERVIEWER: Boy, you hell!

SLICK: So we stayed together about a year after that until she just started giving a weird vibe, or like slacking off on sending money for me to go to store, slacking off on visitation and wanting to do other stuff that didn't have nothing to do with me. So that's when I told her she can just go head on and stopped calling her. From there that's when we broke it off after being together for 5 years.

INTERVIEWER: It sounds like she was messing around or like something else had her attention. Did you ever get to the bottom of it?

SLICK: I believe she was messing with someone else. Even though she denied it, I was able to verify she was. For instance, like when you go back and look at stuff like certain post on Instagram, because during this time, IG was kind of new and bear in mind I didn't have a phone nor was I on Instagram at the time, but when I did get up to speed, I made a page and went on hers and checked her old posts around the time we broke up and she posted something about this new guy or whatever and it was just too close in time to when we broke up for me to think she wasn't messing with this dude prior to her posting this. It was like they already in love three months after we just broke up from being together after five years? Nall, you been messing with this person.

INTERVIEWER: I feel you on that!

SLICK: But the even more ironic part is that after a year of not being with her, the people went ahead and paroled me out eight months ahead of the scheduled date.

INTERVIEWER: She might not have been any good for you in the grand scheme of things.

SLICK: We gotta pay attention to the signs.

LOGGING OUT

A lot of men behind the wall just pray that people in society can realize that they are everyday people who love, who get sad, who hurt, who are happy, and who have dreams. Each story was a depiction of the various ways this is expressed while one is in a suppressed environment. "You can lock us up. But you can't stop us from being a human being." Mr. Rockhard, Jack Game, Fight or Fuck, Fetty, and Slick are all black men who were incarcerated when they were really young. This is what the data tends to show as it pertains to black men but what the data doesn't show is who these men are and the effect imprisonment has had on them as human beings.

LOADING

ABOUT THE AUTHOR

MALIK IBN LEROW, CONVICT advisor, entrepreneur, and retail trader who served over a decade behind bars in the Georgia penal system is the founder of brands Slick Chisel Fitness and Chisel'd Supplements. These brands encourage active living and healthy nutrition to combat obesity and heart disease. He is the author of "The 6 Figure Prisoner" and is dubbed Alpha Convict because of his strong example for at risk youth and the millions of people under correctional supervision nationwide. Malik is a published model and actor who can be found on Instagram @alphacon_model.

LOGGING OFF

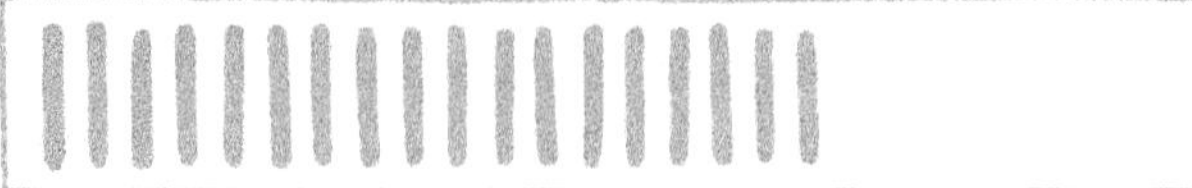